CLARA HUMBLE

HUMBLE

Quiz Whiz

CLARA HUMBLE

Quiz Whiz

Anna Humphrey

Illustrations by Lisa Cinar

Owlkids Books

Owlkids Books acknowledges the financial support of the Canada Council for the Arts, the Ontario Arts Council, the Government of Canada through the Canada Book Fund (CBF), and the Government of Ontario through the Ontario Media Development Corporation's Book Initiative for our publishing activities.

Published in Canada by
Owlkids Books Inc.
10 Lower Spadina Avenue
Toronto, ON M5V 2Z2

Published in the United States by
Owlkids Books Inc.
1700 Fourth Street
Berkeley, CA 94710

Library and Archives Canada Cataloguing in Publication

Humphrey, Anna, 1979-, author
       Clara Humble : quiz whiz / written by
Anna Humphrey ; illustrations by Lisa Cinar.

ISBN 978-1-77147-215-9 (hardback)

       I. Cinar, Lisa, 1980-, illustrator II. Title.

PS8615.U457C528 2017   jC813'.6   C2017-900003-9

Library of Congress Control Number: 2016962527

Edited by: Sarah Howden
Designed by: Barb Kelly

Manufactured in Altona, MB, Canada, in March 2017, by Friesens Corporation
Job #231138

A   B   C   D   E   F

Publisher of Chirp, chickaDEE and OWL
www.owlkidsbooks.com

Owlkids Books is a division of

For Elliot: My Favorite Boy
— A. H.

For Jude Vinalhaven:
the amazing-reading-ninja-wizard!
— L. C.

Contents

The BIG News

Here's a question for you: True or false? Cats are more intelligent than dogs.

If you ask me, the answer is "true," but it's tricky because it depends on what you mean by "intelligent."

Take @Cat, for example, the computerized cat hero of the comic book series I've been writing since I was seven. No, she can't be trained to roll over, fetch a toy, or shake a paw like a dog can, but aren't those activities kind of pointless when you really stop to think about it?

Fetch, kitty!

If that tasteless rubber hamburger is so great, why don't you go get it, buddy?

Plus, refusing to hunt down a squeaky hamburger toy on command doesn't mean she's not intelligent. It just means she's a master of strategy. She knows when to put her impressive intelligence, state-of-the-art circuitry, and unstoppable cuteness to use. And for better or worse, she can even be a little bit cunning and, dare I say, catty, if that's what it takes to win.

Which, now that I think about it, reminds me of what happened when *Smarty Pants*, the world's best TV quiz show for kids, came to town …

Ever since my dad got a job working afternoons at the H&H hardware store, I'd been going to my best friend Bradley's house after school. We were in his living room when we heard the incredible news that our all-time-favorite TV quiz show would be filming in our area. It was four o'clock on the dot, and we were secretly eating more Wheat Yummies crackers and cheese while Bradley's nanny, Svetlana, was in the dining room vacuuming up the crumbs from our first snack of Wheat Yummies crackers and cheese.

I remember the crackers, because we always ate Wheat Yummies. (They were guaranteed sesame-seed-free, and sesame seeds make Bradley's tongue itch.) And I remember Svetlana's vacuuming, because we had to turn the volume way up to hear the *Smarty Pants* theme song. It has a head-bopping calypso beat and is one of the best parts of the show. Actually, *all* the parts of *Smarty Pants* are kind of the best.

For one thing, the host, Mitch O'Toole, is what my used-to-be neighbor, Momo, would call "a real card." That's an old-person way of saying totally unique, out there, and one of a kind. His hair is twice the size of his head, he makes puns so bad they make my dad's jokes seem funny, and he wears a different tie every single episode—each one crazier than the last.

Second, kids can learn so much from tuning in to *Smarty Pants*. For example:

1. How many hearts does an octopus have? Is it: A–0, B–1, C–3, or D–9?

2. Which country is the world's leading banana grower? Is it: A–the United States, B–India, C–Denmark, or D–Argentina?

3. How long does a solar eclipse last? Is it: A–7 seconds, B–7 minutes, C–7 hours, or D–7 days?

(Among zillions of other facts, kids who watch *Smarty Pants* would know that the answers are B, B, and B.)

But without a doubt, what makes *Smarty Pants* the hands-down best game show on TV is that to win it, kids need to be so much more than smart. They also need to be fast, fit, and fearless, because the contestants never know what's going to get thrown at them—sometimes literally.

That afternoon, as the theme song ended, Bradley and I both leaned forward so we wouldn't miss a word.

"What's on his tie today?" Bradley squinted. "Are those ... aliens?"

"I think they're palm trees."

The camera finally zoomed in.

"Broccoli!" we both said at the same time.

"Hello, kids, and welcome to another episode of—" Mitch O'Toole cupped a hand around one ear and leaned toward the audience members, waiting for it.

"*SMARTY PANTS!*" they yelled at the top of their lungs. This was followed by lots of screaming and high-fiving. Meanwhile, the contestants stood—bright-eyed and beaming—on glistening golden podiums. Each was covered from head to toe in a shiny silver outfit called a Smart Suit. Finally, Mitch got the crowd under control.

"And now, without further ado, it's time for our first challenge." BA-RUMP-A-BUM-BUM! The challenge music played, and the curtains behind the contestants parted with a velvety swish. "Today's first category is 'The Natural World,' and the topic is 'Wetlands,'" Mitch said. Then, with a big wink, he added, "Try not to get bogged down by it, kids."

The studio audience groaned.

"Oh man." Bradley nibbled nervously on a sesame-free cracker. "This one's gonna be messy."

He was right. The parted curtains had revealed a giant pit filled with what looked like mud.

"Hop in, kids," Mitch instructed the contestants. "And don't forget your safety goggles. As you answer questions, you'll wade through this shoulder-deep mud. If you reach the finish line before the buzzer sounds, you'll score five points. But for each incorrect answer ..." He trailed off ominously. "Well, we'll just have to see what the swamp has in store."

The starting bell sounded and the camera came in for a close-up as the kids lowered themselves into the mud. It looked like chocolate pudding mixed with cat litter.

"Kathy," Mitch said to one contestant, "are you ready for your first question?" Kathy had blonde hair that was sticking out the front of her Smart Suit hood. It was so long, it was already trailing in the mud.

"I'm ready, Mitch," she answered, pumping one fist in the air to show how excited she was. Her friends in the studio audience went wild.

"To which group of animals do frogs belong? Are they: A—amphibians, B—mammals, C—reptiles, or D—*Homo sapiens*?"

"Oh, please!" I shouted at the TV. "That's so easy. Amphibians."

"Amphibians," the girl answered. There was a dinging sound to let everyone know that she was right.

The next girl correctly answered a question about blue herons, and the girl after that knew a lot about the breeding habits of mosquitoes. The first boy contestant wasn't nearly as quick and clever, though.

"Toby," Mitch said, "peat is commonly found in bogs. But what is peat, exactly? Is it: A—an accumulation of partially decayed vegetation, B—a type of moss, C—an important source of fuel in some parts of the world, or D—all of the above?"

The boy didn't even stop to think, which is a fatal mistake in *Smarty Pants*—especially when you get a question with an "all of the above" option. At least half the time, that's the right one to choose.

"The answer's B, Mitch," he proclaimed. "A type of moss."

BZZZZZT. The wrong-answer buzzer went off.

"I bet they're going to throw rubber frogs at him," Bradley said.

It was a good guess. But what the bog had in store was much muckier. A huge gush of the same gross mixture fell from above, splashing onto the kid's head and coating him so thickly, you could hardly see his Smart Suit anymore.

"Ooooooh!" Bradley and I both shouted at the same time.

"I'm sorry, Toby. It looks like you've been swamp-slimed!" Mitch said. The audience laughed as Toby wiped his goggles clean on the sleeve of his Smart Suit. "The correct answer was D, all of the above."

"Of course it was," I groaned.

"Now it's time for our first commercial break," Mitch went on. "Don't move a muscle, kids. We'll be riiiiiiight back."

And that was when it happened. Svetlana turned off the vacuum cleaner, sending a hush through Bradley's house, and at the same moment, *Smarty Pants* cut to a pretaped segment and Mitch O'Toole spoke the single most exciting sentence I had ever heard in my entire life. With the TV volume still turned all the way up, his words echoed off Bradley's living room walls.

In my excitement, I actually spit part of my cracker onto the rug. I'd have to remember to clean that up later, or Svetlana was *not* going to be happy.

"Do you think you've got what it takes to be a contestant on *Smarty Pants*?" Mitch went on. "If so, come on down to the Gleason Community Center on Saturday, April 10, at 11:30 a.m. for auditions. You could earn a chance to participate in the live taping of *Smarty Pants*. And if you're our winner of the week, you'll take home a thousand-dollar *cash prize*. That's right! *One thousand dollars!* Plus the right to call yourself the smartest kid in your city."

"Bradley! Clara! Lower the volume," Svetlana shouted.

But we didn't move a muscle. Like great blue herons hunting prey in the wetlands (thank you, *Smarty Pants*), we were perfectly motionless. Totally transfixed.

Mitch held up his necktie, which was covered in pictures of cartoon eyeballs. "I'll see *you* at the auditions," he said. Then he winked at the camera—but I swear, it was like he was looking *right* at me.

"Excuse me." Svetlana stood in the doorway. Her blue eyeliner was especially curvy at the sides that day, and that, combined with the tight line of her mouth, made her look fierce, like an Egyptian warrior princess wielding a vacuum. "Bradley Cameron Degen, what did I just ask you?"

Bradley picked up the remote and lowered the volume, but he didn't even say sorry, which just goes to show how distracted he was. Bradley is always polite.

"Are you thinking what I'm thinking?" he asked once Svetlana had given up waiting for an apology and left, dragging the vacuum behind her.

"Yes!" I nearly squealed. I grabbed one of his mom's frilly throw cushions and hugged it so hard, I thought the stuffing might pop out. "True or false?" I grinned at Bradley. "Clara Humble is about to become world famous and win *one thousand dollars.*"

Bradley was quiet for a second. Then all of a sudden, he started coughing. I figured he was probably choking on some cracker crumbs, so I whacked him helpfully on the back before handing him his glass of water.

"So?" I prompted when he'd caught his breath.

He looked at me kind of blankly—which made me worry that maybe I'd whacked him a little too hard, causing his brain to skip a beat.

"What do you think? True or false?" I said again.

"Oh, true," he said softly.

For a split second, his reaction worried me. Didn't he believe I could win? Bradley and I had been watching *Smarty Pants* together for almost a year. I always got the answers right. And much like @Cat, I was cunning, quick, and unafraid of adversity (whether it came in the form of plastic frogs, green slime, or anything else Mitch O'Toole might have up his sleeve).

Of course, then I remembered that Bradley is always practical. He was probably just thinking about the hard work involved in winning—and, of course, he was right. It wasn't going to be easy. Still, being a winner starts with having a winning attitude.

"Definitely true," I corrected him. After all, nobody (except for maybe @Cat) had a more winning attitude than me. "You'll help me study, right?"

When it came to getting organized, thinking ahead, and keeping track of the details, my best friend was unbeatable. Behind every superhero there's a superb sidekick.

"Sure." Bradley gave me a small smile. "I always help you, right?"

This was true. Whether he was coaching me to strengthen the superpowers I'd thought I had near the beginning of the school year, giving me helpful feedback on how to make @Cat more awesome, or just reminding me that we had French homework, Bradley always had my back.

And that was how I knew for almost certain that fame and game-show fortune would soon be mine.

The Competition Heats Up

A thousand dollars is a lot of money. In fact, the possibilities for what you can buy with it are almost endless. You could get a thousand cans of orange soda, twenty thousand gummy candies at the convenience store, about a hundred new books … or if you use one of those discount travel websites, maybe even a vacation to Waikiki!

But while all those things would be nice, none of them can make a person happy forever. That's because true, lasting happiness comes from sharing your gifts with others—which was exactly what I planned to do after I became the next *Smarty Pants* winner of the week and took home fistfuls of cash.

To be clear, though, I wasn't planning to give my prize money away to UNICEF or one of those charities that knits tiny sweaters for penguins after oil spills (not that those aren't both great things). What I had in mind was more along the lines of sharing my considerable *talents* with the world, and I already knew just how I was going to do it: by publishing my comics and making them available to my (soon-to-be) adoring public.

It was Tiffany Jones's aunt Terry who first gave me the idea. She had visited our class right before Halloween, brought us some spooky spider cupcakes, and talked about being a cookbook writer. While we ate, she told us how she'd published her own recipe book by printing copies off the internet.

I looked it up online, and it was true! If you sent your finished draft to www.print-my-book-right-now.com, you could print a whole book for just five dollars a copy! Using my mom's calculator, I'd already figured out that with a thousand dollars, I could print two hundred copies of *@Cat: Doggy Decimator*—my next and (in my humble opinion) greatest @Cat comic book yet.

And that wasn't even the best part. If I had two hundred copies of such an action-packed comic book, I could easily sell them for ten dollars each. Now, prepare yourself, because the math is about to get tricky. By selling those two hundred books,

I'd make two thousand dollars—doubling my original prize money! Amazing, right? But why stop there?! If I kept going, I could use my two thousand dollars to print four hundred books. And when I sold those for ten dollars each, I'd make four thousand dollars!

200 comic books @ $10 each =

$2,000 Dollars =

400 comics =

THAT'S A WHOLE LOTTA MOOLA!!

$4,000 Dollars ←

If I just kept making and selling comic books, I could easily be a millionaire by the time I turned thirteen.

But even though I had my eye on the cash prize—and the fame and fortune that would follow—I knew I'd need to study hard to win. That was why I got started the second I got home from Bradley's. Well, okay, maybe not the *exact* second. First, I video-messaged with Momo at her retirement community to tell her the amazing news that I was going to audition. She was so excited for me that she did a little dance around the common room with her friend Gerta, then she high-fived the laptop screen so hard she accidentally knocked the computer over.

Once we'd finished our video chat, I downloaded the audition form off the *Smarty Pants* website and brought it to my dad to sign. Then I called my mom at work to tell her all about my plans to publish @Cat. But after all that, I reserved three trivia books through the public library website— which I figured was a great start.

It was a good thing I was so committed to preparing too, because when I got to school the next morning, I found out I wasn't the only one who was determined to get a spot on the show.

As soon as Bradley and I stepped off the bus, I caught a glimpse of the bright red silk flower attached to my friend Abby's favorite floppy sun hat.

"Clara! Bradley! Did you hear the news?" Abby

squeaked in her teeny-tiny voice, which I've always thought was how a mouse would sound if mice could talk. "*Smarty Pants* is holding auditions in Gleason! In two and a half weeks!"

I wasn't surprised she was so excited. Abby was usually pumped about something—whether it was an announcement about a new school gardening club or an opportunity to help a teacher wash the blackboards.

"Are you guys trying out? Because I definitely am," she said.

That didn't surprise me either. Because Abby was a full foot shorter than any other kid in our grade and had that tiny voice, people sometimes assumed she was weak or shy. But then— BLAMMO!—she'd haul an entire bag of medicine balls out of the storage room for Coach Donahue or march up to John Connolly (the biggest bully in the fourth grade) and force him to apologize to the kindergarten kid whose kitty-cat hoodie he'd just made fun of. She was definitely going to be a worthy opponent.

"I'm trying out, but Bradley's not," I explained. "It's not really his thing."

Bradley shrugged as if agreeing. Ever since we were little, he'd hated being the center of attention. It was why he always let me take the biggest speaking parts when we did group presentations, and why he always asked if I would help him blow out the candles on his birthday cake—well, that and because I happen to be a really good candle-blower.

True story: At Bradley's seventh birthday party, I accidentally blew the icing right off the cake.

"Will and Roger are trying out too," Abby added breathlessly.

I gulped. Will and Roger were mathletes, and they were both on the track team, which gave them the added bonus of being coordinated and having stamina.

"Becky McDougall and her friends said they might too," Abby continued. "They think being on TV is a good way to get spotted by a talent agent." She rolled her eyes when she said that, and I didn't blame her.

Bossy Becky was my least favorite student from our rival school, R.R. Reginald. (Unfortunately, R.R. Reginald got infested with mold near the beginning of the school year, and all the students had moved into our building while theirs was being fixed. We'd been stuck with them for almost seven months, and there was no end in sight.)

Since the second she'd arrived, Becky had been acting like she owned the place, and her popularity had been almost instant. A whole bunch of girls in the fourth grade (even the ones from Gledhill, who should have had higher standards) tried to copy her lunches, her outfits, and her opinions. But when it came to *Smarty Pants*, Becky was hardly a threat. Let's just say she wasn't the type to mess up her pretty hair wading through a mud pit.

"I bet a lot of other people are going to try out too," Abby went on. "Everyone's talking about it."

She was right. That day, I must have heard the words "smarty pants" come out of twenty different kids' mouths. It was mostly the ones you'd expect: the kids who were always first to raise their hands, and who tried out for the lead role in the school play. But there was one major exception …

Shane Biggs was—to my supreme disappointment—my new neighbor. After Momo moved away, he and his mom had moved in, torn out all her old kitchen cabinets, repainted everything a dreary color called "storm gray," and ruined Momo's beautiful garden by forgetting to water it. But those weren't even the *real* reasons I didn't like Shane.

I'd tried to give him a chance, but he was majorly negative. He seemed determined to hate everything at Gledhill Elementary. He said that our teachers were too strict and that our field trip to Safety Village was lame, even though we got to drive tiny cars. He even complained about Pepperoni Pizza Fridays (not enough pepperoni) and about the pencil sharpener in Mrs. Smith's class, which he said made the pencils too pointy.

Listening to him complain was always annoying, but that day in gym class his whining reached new heights. We were in the middle of our dance unit, and as we stood against the wall, waiting for Coach Donahue to pair us up for salsa lessons, I overheard Shane talking to this kid Jason, who was pretty much the only person at our school he was friends with.

"When I go on *Smarty Pants* and win first prize," Shane said with a boogery sniff, "the first thing I'm going to buy is a plane ticket back to California. I can live with my grandma. I don't even care that her house smells like cat pee. As long as I don't have to go to *this* school anymore."

"That's just sad," Bradley whispered to me.

"Tell me about it," I whispered back. "Even when he's talking about winning a thousand dollars, he finds a way to complain about our school."

"At my old school, we never had to dance with *girls*," Shane whined to Jason.

"Bradley, you're with Clara," Coach Donahue said, calling out the dance partners. "Angela's with Will. Aimee's with Rob. Jason's with Adila."

As she called out our names, each couple had

to find a spot on the dance floor. Before long, there was almost no one left against the wall. "And Shane's with Becky," the coach said when they were the last two remaining.

"No way!" Shane crossed his arms over his chest. "I'm *not* dancing with Becky McDougall."

Even from across the gym, I could see Becky's cheeks go pink with embarrassment, then promptly deepen to a much scarier shade of red as her rage set in.

"I'm not dancing with *any* girl," Shane added.

"Me neither," his friend Jason said. Adila, who was supposed to be his partner, stared down at her sneakers.

Coach Donahue crossed her arms. "Maybe you two would like to dance together, then," she suggested to Shane and Jason. "And Becky and Adila can partner up."

"Not a chance!" Shane said. "If I dance with Jason, one of us will have to be the *girl*."

He said it like he couldn't imagine a worse fate, but—hello—girls are awesome. Plus, in salsa, they get to do all the spins and stuff.

"In that case," Coach Donahue replied in an

extremely no-nonsense tone, "you'll dance with the partners I've assigned you, or you'll dance your way down to the office. Your choice."

Shane was stubborn, but he wasn't stupid. He waited until Coach Donahue's back was turned before he grumbled to Jason, "Gross. And of all the girls, I get Becky!"

"Watch out she doesn't try to kiss you!" Jason made smoochy lips.

Judging by the look of disgust on Becky's face, I didn't think Shane had anything to worry about.

"Okay guys," Coach Donahue said, clapping her hands. "Let's salsa!" She hit *Play* and started clapping in time with the music. "Quick, quick, slow. Quick, quick, slow."

Not to brag, but Bradley and I were naturals. We floated across the gym floor, swaying our hips to the music and even adding a fancy spin or two for possible extra credit. Matteo and Siu were keeping up, and Angela and Will were kind of getting the hang of it … but the rest of the class wasn't quite feeling the sweet salsa beat.

Aimee and Rob had the hold right, but their footwork was all mixed up. And Glenn and Jamila somehow managed to dance into a wall.

Of all the couples in the gym, though, Shane and Becky were the only true dance disaster. For one thing, they were both refusing to touch or look at each other, so they kept dancing off in different directions. Plus they seemed to have no idea what the steps were.

"Becky and Shane," Coach Donahue called out, "hand-to-hand and hand-to-shoulder."

But they still didn't make actual physical contact until she walked over and placed them in the correct salsa position.

"Ew. Your hands are all sweaty," we heard Becky complain as we glided past.

"You think *that's* gross? I'm pretty sure I just swallowed one of your hairs." Shane made a sputtering sound as he freed one hand to wipe at the corners of his mouth.

"Ew," Becky said again. "Now you've got drool *and* sweat on your hand. I'm *not* touching it until you wash it."

But Becky should have known better. Shane reached toward her with his sweaty-drool hand. She jumped back, forgetting the first rule of dance etiquette Coach Donahue had taught us: be aware of your space. Matteo and Siu were dancing by at just the wrong moment.

"Whoa!" Becky stumbled over Matteo's foot.

She reached forward for something to grab onto, but the only thing within grabbing distance happened to be Shane. He tried to yank his arm away before it could be contaminated by girl cooties, but he was a second too late. Becky caught him with a death grip, and they both went down, tumbling onto the gym floor with their arms and legs tangled together.

"Look, everyone! Becky's hugging Shane!" Will called out, and they scrambled apart like they'd been scalded by each other's touch.

Coach Donahue sighed and stopped the music. "Shane? Becky? Everyone okay?" she asked.

"Oh, great!" Shane yelled, getting up and taking something out of his back pocket. "She made me fall on my cell phone. The screen's all smashed!"

"I didn't make you do anything!" Becky snapped. "*You're* the one who made *me* fall." She started to whimper, holding her left wrist in her right hand.

"Shane, what are you doing with a cell phone in

the gym?" Coach Donahue asked as she walked over to Becky and started examining her wrist.

Our school has a strict no-technology-in-class policy, which is kind of dumb if you ask me. @Cat would be the first to tell you that embracing technology only makes us stronger by keeping us connected. But rules are rules.

Have you been wearing that adorable antenna cozy I knit you?

Yes, Gr&cat.

@Cat takes a break from fighting crime to have a virtual chat with her dear old granny.

"It's for educational purposes," Shane said. "I'm studying for the *Smarty Pants* audition with the Quiz-It app. At recess and stuff. Not during class."

The *Quiz-It app*? I'd never heard of it before. Then again, I wasn't lucky enough to have my own cell phone. Shane, meanwhile, seemed to have all the latest gadgets—including his own laptop, a high-definition TV the size of our dinner table, and three different video game systems.

"You know the rules, Shane," Coach Donahue said. "If you bring an electronic device from home, it stays in your backpack. Go put it away. You'll need to explain to your mother how it got broken."

Shane glanced up from his smashed phone and shot Becky a dirty look. "Yeah, I'll tell my mom how it broke," he grumbled. "Stupid girls. Always wrecking everything."

"Stupid boys is more like it!" Becky retorted— and she didn't even bother to say it quietly. Coach Donahue was getting her to flex her wrist back and forth, which she did with a pained expression. "If this is a sprain, you're *so* going to pay, Shane Biggs!"

Coach Donahue sighed. "That's enough, you two," she said. She let Joanna take Becky to the nurse's office, then she turned the salsa music back on.

"Bradley," I said, once we were moving across the floor again, "make a mental note. We need to get the Quiz-It app for my training. Do you think we can borrow Svetlana's cell phone to download it after school?"

"I don't know," Bradley said. "She's pretty attached to her phone. I'll ask." He shrugged, then he spun me around and we fell back into step flawlessly. "Anyway, it doesn't matter. Even if we can't get that app, I'm pretty sure Shane will never top you in trivia."

I nodded modestly. I mean, what other nine-year-old can list the capitals of every country in the world (in alphabetical order or going from east to west), say who conquered the Aztec empire, and name the inventor of the can opener? Practically none. That's how many!

"But we'll need to prepare you for the physical challenges," Bradley went on as we sailed past Glenn and Jamila, who had managed to dance into another wall.

"I'm on the track team *and* I play intramural basketball at lunch sometimes," I pointed out. "Plus you can't get much more coordinated than this." I did a lock-twirl hand switch to prove my point.

"But have you tried doing those things while answering trivia questions?" Bradley asked, swinging me back into position. "And then there's math."

I sighed heavily. He was right. I had a hard enough time when Mrs. Smith called me up to the board to do long division. How was I expecting to answer math questions while slogging through mud, climbing a ten-foot wall, finding my way through a shifting maze, or doing whatever other crazy challenge Mitch O'Toole might throw at me?

"Don't worry," Bradley said. "I'm already planning your training schedule. By the time we're done, you'll be doing long division on a tightrope in your sleep."

Tightrope sleep-math? It's doubtful that @Cat herself could pull off such a daring feat–even with her built-in calculator function!

I didn't exactly believe it, but I hoped Bradley was right. The auditions were still two and a half weeks away, and the competition was already heating up. I was going to need all the help I could get.

Winner in Training

Even though we begged and pleaded, Svetlana said we couldn't use her cell phone to download the Quiz-It app. I was hoping my dad might let me use his phone when I got home, but in the meantime, I tried to make the most of the time we had after school that day. While Bradley was hard at work setting up my training circuit in the backyard, I sat with his little sister, Val, and watched that day's episode of *Smarty Pants*.

I could hear Bradley moving things around outside the window, but I made a supreme effort not to peek. (After all, being surprised by the challenges would be part of the real game.)

When the show ended, I poked my head out the back door.

There was Bradley, pedaling Val's tricycle in tight circles.

"I've tested everything," he said, catching sight

of me and coming to a stop. "I'm pretty sure we're ready." He got off the trike and motioned for me to take his place. "Wait! First you need to put these on." He handed me a pair of safety goggles. "I borrowed them from Stuart's pile of junk."

Stuart was Bradley's mom's new boyfriend. She'd met him only a few months before, but he already kept an electric toothbrush and a shaving kit in their bathroom. Also, he was storing a whole bunch of stuff in their garage because his basement had flooded.

It wasn't as if Bradley went in the garage much, but for some reason, Stuart's stuff still drove him crazy. Most things about Stuart did—especially his habit of giving advice nobody had asked for. Stuart even had a series of videos he'd made and posted on the internet. They were called "Stuart's Six Secrets to Success."

"I borrowed a few other things too," Bradley said.

I looked around the yard. It seemed as if Bradley had borrowed *everything*. The winter tires from Stuart's sports car were placed around the lawn. His screwdrivers and hammers were hanging from the branches of the blossoming crabapple tree. And a ton of sporting equipment—mostly life jackets and hockey pads—was piled inside the giant hole that Bradley and I had made near his garage while doing our most recent archaeological dig.

"Do I really have to wear these?" I asked, holding up the safety goggles.

"Do you want to win?" Bradley asked. He could see the answer in my eyes. "Then you have to wear them. The kids on the show wear safety goggles in every round. It's important to make the training as close to the real thing as possible."

He dug around in a shopping bag on the picnic table and pulled out three jars. One was filled with those candied cherries that go on the tiny swords in Shirley Temples. They were floating in bright pink water. Another jar had applesauce in it. And the third looked like it held some kind of spicy pickles.

"Don't tell me you're planning to dump that stuff on me," I said.

He smiled. "Only if you get a wrong answer."

I knew there was no use arguing. Bradley had a vision, and he wasn't going to be happy unless we did it just right.

"I borrowed this from Stuart's junk too," he said,

Feliz Navidad...

taking a tie out of his shopping bag. He strung it around his neck, then touched a star to show how the little lights on its Christmas tree blinked while the tie played a tinny-sounding version of "Feliz Navidad."

The only thing missing was Mitch O'Toole's giant hair—or so I thought. Once again, Bradley reached into the shopping bag, and this time he pulled out a rainbow clown wig. He put it on and tucked a few stray bits of hair underneath.

"Hello, kids," he said, grinning from ear to ear, "and welcome to another episode of—" He cupped a hand around one ear and leaned toward me, just like Mitch O'Toole.

"SMARTY PANTS!" I yelled, because I knew he wasn't going to go on until I did.

Bradley flipped open a notebook. "Our first category today is 'History', and the topic is 'Locomotion.' Contestant, please put on your safety goggles and get onto the tricycle."

He handed me a helmet. I rolled my eyes as I did up the strap.

"For your first challenge, you must ride around this giant hole ten times before the buzzer sounds. Are you ready?"

I pedaled across the grass toward the giant hole, which—let me tell you—was not as easy as it sounds. For one thing, Bradley's lawn was pretty bumpy. And for another, the tricycle was way too small for me. My knees were almost hitting my chin.

Luckily, I'm no quitter. "Ready!" I shouted.

"On your mark. Get set. Go!" Bradley yelled.

I started to pedal furiously.

"When was the First Transcontinental Railroad, also known as the Pacific Railroad, built? Was it: A—in 1910, B—between 2006 and 2009, C—between 1863 and 1869, or D—in 1920?"

When you're not sure of an answer, it's important not to rush. I considered the possibilities while I did my first loop of the hole.

"C," I shouted back. It was easy when I stopped to think about it. Everyone knows railroads are really old, so it couldn't have been built between 2006 and

2009. And obviously it would take more than a year to construct an entire railroad, so that meant A and D were out. C was the only possible answer.

"Correct!" Bradley said. "Next question: Name the human-powered mode of transport that is a two-wheeled cart pulled by a runner. Is it: A—a dolly, B—a pedicab, C—a tuk-tuk, or D—a rickshaw?"

I didn't even need to think about that one. My mom and I rode one once in the market in Ottawa.

"D—a rickshaw," I yelled, but I must have run over a rock in the grass or something, because as I went into my third loop, the front wheel of the trike veered sharply to the left, nearly sending me tumbling into the hole. Even though it was padded with life jackets and hockey pads, it was still pretty deep. Thankfully, I managed to jerk the handlebars back to the right and make a full recovery.

Bradley went on to the next question. "The first monster truck was built in 1979 in Missouri. Was its name: A—*Monster Mash*, B—*Big Foot*, C—*Car Crusher*, or D—*Bob*?"

A monster truck question? I didn't know the first thing about monster trucks. I was going to have to make a guess, and the sooner the better. I was only on my fifth lap, and I was already out of breath.

"C," I said with as much energy as I could muster. *"Car Crusher."*

Just then, I looked through the small back window of the garage and saw someone moving around inside. I could tell it was Stuart by the glare of the super-big mirrored sunglasses he liked to wear. The doorknob started to turn, but Bradley was too busy consulting the answer sheet to notice.

"Bzzzzzt! Sorry, Clara!" he shouted. "The correct answer is B—*Big Foot*!" He walked to the picnic table and picked up the jar of cherries.

I knew my penalty was coming (and it was going to be sticky), so I started pedaling faster, hoping to dodge it. Unfortunately, that meant I wasn't paying enough attention to where I was going. The front wheel of the trike hit the same rock as before, and this time … "Oof!" I flopped into the hole with the trike on top of me, then watched as an arc of bright pink water sailed above me.

"Braaaaadley!" Stuart's voice boomed a second later.

I struggled to free my legs from the trike and pull

myself out of the hole, shaking off a life jacket that was stuck to my arm.

Stuart—who had stepped out the back door of the garage at just the wrong moment—was standing with his hands on his hips. Maraschino-cherry water stained the front of his white shirt and dripped off the ends of his mustache.

"Oops," Bradley said.

Oops was right. And I wasn't even talking about Stuart getting cherried—although that was a problem too. I'd messed up on my third question and fallen into the giant hole on my sixth lap. In the real game, that would have meant missing five points for the question, plus five additional points for failing to complete the challenge. Clearly, I still had a lot of work ahead of me.

"What's the big idea here?" Stuart said. He lifted up his sunglasses to get a look at his ruined shirt, then caught sight of a few other things. "Is that my Ab-Flex Deluxe?" He pointed to a complicated-looking piece of exercise equipment on the other side of the lawn. "And my vintage vinyl record collection?!"

Bradley had tied string through the middle of the big black discs and strung them at different lengths along the clothesline. I was guessing they were going to be part of an obstacle course—but now I'd never find out.

"Clean this up, Bradley," Stuart said through gritted teeth. You could tell he was trying hard to keep his cool, but the ends of his mustache were twitching with anger. "I want everything back in its place, and your mother *will* be hearing about this." Then he marched into the house and let the screen door slam behind him.

Audition Day

Over the next two and a half weeks, I trained with Bradley every chance I got—but we didn't dare borrow Stuart's stuff again.

While other kids were talking and telling jokes on the bus, I was juggling beanbags and doing multiplication drills. While they played wall ball at recess, I crab-walked around the track-and-field oval, answering questions about sea crustaceans. While my parents chilled out watching TV after dinner, I was in Bradley's backyard, running blindfolded around traffic cones and shouting out the names of state capitals.

In fact, pretty much the only time I wasn't training for *Smarty Pants* was when I was sleeping (unless you counted the nights I was *dreaming* about *Smarty Pants*).

We also couldn't train on Saturdays. That was frustrating. After all, those were the only days when Bradley and I could have had completely uninterrupted time, since he had church on Sundays. But after he borrowed Stuart's stuff without asking, accidentally threw cherry water at him, and then refused to apologize sincerely, Stuart gave Bradley's mom some unasked-for advice.

"He says I need a strong male influence in my life," Bradley had complained the day after the Maraschino Mustache Mishap, as we began calling it. "Now he wants us to spend every Saturday together, bonding. It's the worst punishment ever."

I tried to sympathize, but honestly, it didn't sound *that* bad. The first Saturday, Stuart had taken Bradley to the go-kart track, and the weekend after that they'd played laser tag.

"He kept sneaking out of the fog and shooting me in the back!" Bradley complained. "What kind of strong male influence is *that*?!"

I didn't say anything, but I was pretty sure that shooting people with a laser was the whole point of laser tag.

Now it was the Saturday after laser tag—the long-awaited day of the *Smarty Pants* auditions, to be exact—and we were sitting on Bradley's front steps, waiting for Stuart to finish waxing his mustache, polishing his mega-huge mirrored sunglasses, or doing whatever else he needed to do to get ready.

"Well," I said, trying to comfort my best friend, "at least you don't have to be alone with Stuart today."

Bradley had managed to convince Stuart that I should come along for that day's bonding activity— cheering on his favorite hockey team at an all-you-can-eat chicken wings restaurant—but only *after* he drove us to the auditions and waited for me to finish.

At first, it seemed like a win-win-win situation: Bradley could bolster my spirits at the auditions, I could save him from having to spend time alone with Stuart, and we could all eat a lot of chicken wings. But then I saw for myself how truly aggravating Stuart could be. It started before we'd even left the driveway.

"Bradley," Stuart said as we climbed into his sports car, which was bright yellow and reminded me of a banana on wheels, "don't you have another pair of jeans?"

Bradley shrugged. "Yeah."

"Well, why don't you run back in and put them on? Those ones have holes in them."

"I like holes," Bradley answered.

There really is a lot to like about holes. For one thing, they keep your legs from overheating. Also, you can use them to draw knee people when you get bored at school.

Fred and Ted: my favorite knee people. They're always teasing each other, but they're really the best of friends.

Hey, Fred. Knee-ner, Knee-ner, Knee-ner!

Ted, you kneed to stop teasing me!

"Suit yourself," Stuart said. "But you know what they say: You never get a second chance to make a first impression. If I were auditioning for a TV show, I'd want to look my best."

"Bradley's not trying out for the show," I pointed out as I checked my reflection in the bananamobile rearview mirror. "Only I am." I had to admit, I looked *extremely* TV-ready. I'd picked out my lucky hair barrettes, my favorite T-shirt, and my best pair of sparkly leggings.

"Really? Why aren't you trying out too, Bradley?" Stuart asked as he backed out of the driveway.

Bradley shrugged again.

"He doesn't want to," I supplied.

Stuart turned to look at us in the backseat. "Doesn't want to, or doesn't believe he can succeed?"

I could tell from the glint in his eye that he was gearing up for a motivational talk.

Stuart's motivational eye glint.

"You know, Bradley, the second of my Six Secrets to Success is to believe in your personal potential."

"Sure," I said, coming to Bradley's defense. "But the first Secret to Success is to know your strengths, right?"

I was by no means a huge fan, but I *had* watched Stuart's videos a time or two—just in case there was something in there that might help me become the world's youngest and most famous published comic book artist.

"Bradley doesn't like everyone watching him," I explained. "He's more of a behind-the-scenes kind of person."

"You know, Bradley"—Stuart glanced at us in the rearview mirror—"to succeed at something new, you first need to try it."

"Sure," Bradley said. Then he looked out the window in a way that made it clear he was barely listening, while Stuart spent the rest of the ride lecturing us about self-esteem and dreams coming true.

When we got to the Gleason Community Center, the parking lot was full and there were cars all up and down the street. Stuart had to let us out at the corner and go find a place to park.

"Are you ready?" Bradley asked as we started up the front steps. There were at least twenty kids our age standing just outside the doors. I recognized a few of them from school, and some from different summer camps I had been to. It didn't faze me, though. So what if there was a little competition? Thanks to Bradley, I was prepared.

Then he opened the main doors and I gasped. The kids were packed in like sardines. (Trivia fact: Those are small, oily fish often sold in cans.) There were so many of them that I had to leave Bradley by the doors and elbow my way through to the registration table.

"Hi!" I said, giving the gray-haired woman behind the table my brightest, smartest smile. "I'm here to meet Mitch O'Toole and audition for *Smarty Pants*."

"You and everyone else in town, apparently." The woman adjusted her tortoiseshell glasses. "Do you have your registration form?"

I took it out of my pocket and put it down in front of her, smoothing out the creases so that it would look extra crisp and professional.

She highlighted a few things and then, with a tight smile, handed me a number. "Make yourself comfortable, sweetie," she said. "It'll be a bit of a wait."

I clutched my number (lucky 77), turned, and

stood on my tiptoes, trying to see through the crowd to find Bradley. He wasn't by the doors where I'd left him, or standing in line for the water fountain, or reading the signs on the bulletin board. I was just about to make my way over to the viewing window for the pool (Bradley loved watching high dives), but before I could make any headway through the crowd, a commotion broke out near the front doors.

Two men were bringing in big lights and a camera, and a familiar woman with super-straight dark brown hair and a microphone in her hand was following them. It was Sarah Barrasson: the announcer my parents always watched on the local news.

"Excuse me," I said, squeezing between two girls who were going over a list of trivia questions. "Pardon me." I turned sideways and scooted past Will and Roger from my school. The camera guy was already hoisting the camera up onto one shoulder, and I was determined to get in the shot so I could tell Momo to tune in and watch for me. I would have made it too, if two boys hadn't pushed past me.

"Who'd like to do a short interview live on the air for the noon news?" Sarah Barrasson asked. Practically every kid in the room put up their hand. "What about one of you young men?" she said to the two boys who'd just butted in front of me.

"Wait! Choose me! I have a natural presence on camera." I turned to see Bossy Becky McDougall striding through the crowd. She had her hair all curled and tied with shiny pink ribbons. She always looked kind of la-di-da, but that day she was la-di-da-di-DA.

"No way! She said she wanted one of us *young men*," said one of the boys, turning back to glare at Becky. It was none other than Shane Biggs. He stepped right in front of the camera without waiting for another invitation.

"And lights … camera … action," said a woman holding a clipboard.

Right on cue, Sarah Barrasson's face lit up like a hundred-watt bulb. "Hi there, *News at Noon* viewers. I'm here at the Gleason Community Center, where auditions are being held for *Smarty Pants*—a game show that invites fourth-graders to answer skill-testing questions and complete challenging tasks for the chance to win one thousand dollars."

As the news announcer talked, I could see Becky's face going redder and redder. Shane was in her spotlight, and it was becoming obvious from the way her lips were twitching that she wasn't going to put up with it.

"And what made you decide to come out to audition for *Smarty Pants* today, young man?" Sarah asked before tilting the microphone toward Shane.

"Well," he started, "for a few months now, I've been answering trivia questions on this app called Quiz-It. I'm constantly beating my own high scores. So I figure I have a good shot. Plus I want to win the thousand dollars."

"Oh, puh-lease," I heard Becky mutter. "What kind of answer is that?" Then, before anyone really knew what was happening—least of all Shane— Becky had pushed her way into the shot and was snatching the microphone from his hand.

I noticed that she was still wearing a tensor bandage on the wrist she'd hurt in the salsa

incident more than two weeks before. According
to Becky, her doctor said it was a "class-two, semi-
serious sprain." I knew, because Becky had told
everyone. Many times. Lots of girls had been
taking turns carrying her books for her, and they
all gave Shane dirty looks whenever they passed
him in the hall.

"Personally," Becky said, tossing her hair over one
shoulder and giving the camera the goody-two-
shoes smile she usually saved for teachers, "I'm
here today because I think being on *Smarty Pants*
is going to be *so educational.*"

Shane tried to grab the microphone back, but
Becky held it tightly in her good hand. She smiled
warmly at the camera, but outside the shot, she
stepped hard on Shane's foot. He yelped and
started hopping around.

It wasn't a gentlemanly thing, but considering
that Becky had just stomped on his toes, I couldn't
exactly blame Shane when he reached around,
grabbed a big handful of her curly blonde hair, and
pulled.

"Ouch! Shane, stop it!" Becky yelled.

Sarah Barrasson had been doing the news for as

long as I could remember. I guess she'd dealt with this kind of thing before.

"Hahahaha," she laughed, as if seeing the people she was interviewing attack each other was a delightful joke. Then she reached over and plucked the microphone from Becky's hand. "Well, it's obvious that the competition is going to be fierce. In fact, it's already like cats and dogs here at the Gleason Community Center."

Becky narrowed her eyes at Shane. "If you ever pull my hair again …" she hissed.

Shane stared back at her with this dopey expression on his face, as if he'd already forgotten what he'd done wrong.

Sarah Barrasson was right—they were exactly like cats and dogs.

I'm pretty sure this is what Shane Biggs would look like in dog form.

FANCY FISH BITES

For cats that believe they deserve the best.

And Becky would definitely be the cat from the Fancy Fish Bites commercial.

"But who will get a spot on *Smarty Pants*? And who will take home the grand prize?" Sarah Barrasson concluded with a smile. "Tune in to find out. And now it's over to Desi Kanagaraj for sports."

As soon as the camera turned off, she groaned and rubbed at her temples. "They don't pay me enough to do this job some days," she said to the woman with the clipboard.

As the TV crew packed up their gear, Becky, Darla, Joanna, and a few other girls congregated near the bulletin boards, whispering furiously while casting menacing glances toward Shane, who was standing to my left with Jason. They were talking in low growls, like they were plotting something.

Thankfully, before things could get even uglier, a

woman in a *Smarty Pants* T-shirt opened the gym doors. "Numbers 66 through 77," she called. "Can I have you line up here, please. That's numbers 66 through 77."

"I'm number 66." Becky held up her number as she flounced toward the door.

Just then, I caught sight of Bradley. "Did you see what just happened?" I said, pushing my way through the crowd. "I can't believe that was on live TV!"

"I only saw the very end of it," he answered. "I was standing in line getting this." He held up a piece of paper with the number 98 on it. He'd already dog-eared the corner a little from rolling it nervously between his fingers.

At first, I stared at him blankly, not understanding what had happened.

"Stuart said I had to try out too," Bradley explained, looking down at his feet. "He even called my mom and got her permission. He says I should put myself out there and take chances."

Stuart and his stupid suggestions! Why couldn't he just leave Bradley alone? He didn't want to be on the show! And it didn't make any sense for both of us to audition. I knew I could beat just about anyone when it came to trivia—but just about anyone didn't include Bradley. He was one of the smartest kids I knew. Plus he was my personal trivia trainer. That meant he knew all the same stuff I did, and maybe even more.

The woman with the clipboard was still standing at the gym door. "Numbers 66 through 77, this is your last call!"

"Clara!" Bradley looked down at the number I was holding. "That's you! You're 77."

My heart started to race. How had I managed to nearly miss my call? Once again, I realized how lucky I was to have Bradley on my side. I knew I didn't *really* have any reason to worry. After all, even though Stuart was forcing him to try out, Bradley wanted me to win.

"I'm coming!" I called, holding up my number. Then I turned back to Bradley and whispered, "Don't worry. Stuart can force you to try out, but he can't make you get a spot, right? When they ask you questions, just get all the answers wrong on purpose. And when they interview you to see if you'd be good on TV, make this face a lot."

My dumbest face.

I started to cross the room, ready to meet Mitch O'Toole.

"Clara!" Bradley called. "Remember everything I taught you, okay?"

I nodded. I knew that, thanks to Bradley, I was as prepared as I could possibly be.

"And when they interview you to see if you'd be good on TV, make this face a lot," he added.

Bradley's smartest face.

I gave my best friend a thumbs-up, then I walked through the door to begin my journey to trivia-show fame and fortune.

The Best Worst News

Charisma. Few possess it, and even fewer understand it. Basically, charisma is a quality that gives someone influence over a large number of people. (I know, because I looked it up in the dictionary as soon as I got home from the auditions.) And not to brag, but I peeked at the judges' score sheets, and I happen to be a five out of five in that area.

I also scored high in "communication skills" and "general likability," not to mention that I'd kicked butt in the written trivia questions *and* I was the first one to finish the crazy obstacle course testing our physical endurance—despite the fact that I selflessly stopped to help Bossy Becky untangle her fancy hair bow when it got stuck to the walls of the Velcro tunnel.

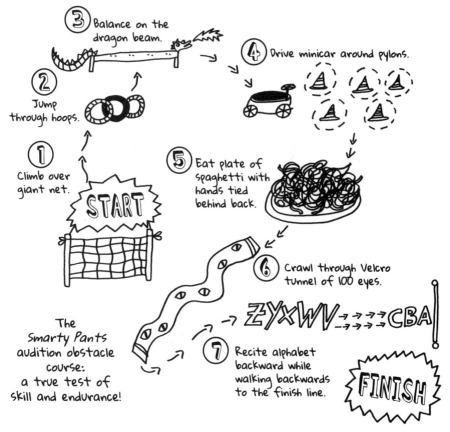

③ Balance on the dragon beam.

② Jump through hoops.

④ Drive minicar around pylons.

① Climb over giant net.

START

⑤ Eat plate of spaghetti with hands tied behind back.

⑥ Crawl through Velcro tunnel of 100 eyes.

The Smarty Pants audition obstacle course: a true test of skill and endurance!

ZYXWV → → → → CBA

⑦ Recite alphabet backward while walking backwards to the finish line.

FINISH

Overall, my audition went great. The only disappointing part was that I didn't get to meet Mitch O'Toole. (I asked where he was, and the interviewer said he never went to the auditions.)

Still, I didn't let that get me down. I was 99 percent sure I was going to get a spot as a contestant, and I knew I had Bradley to thank for that. Unfortunately, he was still mad at Stuart, and he was in no mood to celebrate.

"In your one-on-one interview, did they start with a question about why you wanted to be on the show?" I asked him.

Bradley nodded. We were sitting in a booth at Chubby Chicken, and the waitress had just put a huge tray of mouthwatering wings in front of us. I chose an especially saucy one off the top, but Bradley just sat there.

"And what was the first question on your written test?" I went on, pushing the plate toward him. "Was it about vampire bats?"

"Yeah." Bradley spun his coaster on its side, then he finally reached over to take a wing. He nibbled it slowly at first, but once he knew how good it was, he couldn't help himself. He ate three in a row and grabbed a fourth.

"That vampire bat one was pretty easy, right?" I said, licking sauce off my fingers. I had to hand it to Stuart. He was kind of annoying, but he knew how to pick a great restaurant. Not only was the food delicious, but it also had those prepackaged lemon wipes for cleaning your hands. And the salt and pepper shakers were shaped like eggs.

"I wasn't so sure about the third one, though,"

I said. "The math question about fractions. I just chose 'all of the above.'"

"It was all of the above," Bradley answered. He looked off to one side to avoid making eye contact with Stuart, who seemed oh-so-pleased with himself for having encouraged Bradley to "Dream Big!"—the third Secret to Success.

"Yes! That means I got them all right!" I pumped my fist in the air at the exact same moment that Stuart's hockey team scored a goal on the big-screen TV. Everyone in the restaurant went wild, almost as if they were celebrating my victory too—everyone, that is, except Bradley.

For several long minutes, we sat there in silence—well, except for the hockey and restaurant noises buzzing around us. At one point, Bradley made a weird face and scrunched up his nose, and a minute or two later he stuck out his tongue and tried to see its reflection on the back of a spoon. But neither one of us realized what was starting to happen until …

"Want to build a castle out of creamers and shoot sugar packets at it?" I asked. Creamer Castle was our favorite restaurant game. We once built a castle so big and so strong that we had to borrow sugar packets from almost every table in the restaurant to conquer it.

"No danks," Bradley said.

"No *danks*?" I repeated.

"I mend, do danks," he said. Then he looked down at the chicken wing in his hand. "Oh doh. Dey had seddame in dem!"

Stuart called the waitress over to check, and sure enough, the wings we'd just devoured had been cooked in 100 percent sesame oil. Stuart got all panicky and called Bradley's mom, but he was worrying for nothing. Bradley had had his sesame thing since he was a little kid. It was called an oral allergy. A few minutes after he ate the seeds, his mouth and tongue got allergic, but the rest of his body was okay.

And actually, it was kind of lucky timing, because it cheered Bradley up a bit. Whenever he accidentally ate sesame seeds and his mouth went crazy, we always tried to make the most of it.

"Okay, try saying 'puddle duck,'" I suggested.

"Duddle buck," Bradley repeated, then he couldn't help smiling.

"Okay, now try 'In my humble opinion.'"

He put on an extra-serious face: "Id my hunble bobinion."

I laughed. Then I glanced around the restaurant, looking for another idea. I finally spotted the perfect thing on a sign near the door:

OUR DRUMSTICKS CAN'T BE BEAT!

"Okay! Okay! Now try 'Our drumsticks can't be beat!'"

He struck the same pose as the cartoon chicken. "Ow bumkicks cam be beat!" he said.

"Bumkicks!" I cracked up so hard I could barely breathe. Stuart had to turn around and apologize to the people at the table behind us.

But I mean, c'mon! Bumkicks? It was comedy gold. In fact, I was laughing so hard that it took me a minute to realize Bradley had gone completely quiet again. When I finally looked up, wiping a tear from my eye, he was staring down at the table, folding his napkin into a little square—and that was when I started to suspect that something was *really* bugging him. Something more than just being mad at Stuart.

I didn't figure out exactly what it was until later in the week, though—on that fateful Tuesday night when the phone rang, I ruined the raisin bran muffins, and everything started to change.

By then, three days had gone by since the auditions, and I'd been watching the mailbox like a hawk (or like the common housefly—which has complete 360-degree vision and up to five hundred lenses in each eye). I was waiting for news from the *Smarty Pants* studio and taking advantage of the last of the afternoon sunlight to work on some pages for my soon-to-be-published comic book.

In @*Cat: Doggy Decimator*, Poodle Noodle (the villainous balloon-animal poodle) is up to no good again. Along with his posse of puppies, he's trying to kill all the plants in the land of Animalea by peeing on them. Soon, every bit of vegetation will shrivel up and die. There will be no blossoms left for the bees to make honey with, no roses for beautiful bouquets, and—gasp!—no catnip.

"Clara?" My mom peeked in from the kitchen. She was wearing an apron with little hearts on it and was busy greasing a muffin tin with a paper towel. That could mean only one thing: it was her turn to bring a coffee-break treat to work the next day. "Have you finished your homework yet?"

"Almost." I glanced out the window. "I'll do the rest soon."

"You know," Mom said, "the letter carrier already came."

"I know," I said, but I didn't leave my spot near the window. After all, what if she'd forgotten a letter in her bag and come back? Stranger things have happened.

① For decades, sightings of Bigfoot have been reported across America.

② In ancient Egypt, workers built massive pyramids using only Stone Age tools.

③ A natural display of colored lights (called the aurora borealis) is sometimes seen in the skies in northern regions.

Just a few things that are stranger than the letter carrier coming twice in one day.

"Okay, but don't sit there too long. Remember, you also need to clean Bijou's cage."

I hadn't forgotten. My pet chinchilla was always chewing up toilet paper rolls and making a huge mess of her cage, and my mom was always reminding me to clean it.

"I won't forget," I promised.

"That's what you said last night—" My mom probably would have launched into one of her "responsible pet owners" speeches, but the phone rang. "Finish your drawing, then straight upstairs to clean the cage, okay?"

She headed for the phone and I turned my attention back to my comic.

"Clara!" she called all of a sudden. "Come here!"

I dropped my sketchbook onto the coffee table and sulked into the kitchen, expecting to get nagged about the dirty dishes I'd left on the counter. But Mom was holding the phone out to me with a grin on her face.

"It's for you," she said.

I put the phone to my ear. "Hello?"

"Clara?" The voice on the other end of the line was big, bubbly, and totally unfamiliar. "My name is Angie Matheson. I'm a producer from *Smarty Pants*."

Instantly, every muscle in my body went tense with anticipation.

"I'm calling to let you know that our judges were really impressed with your audition."

She spoke in such a loud voice that I found myself holding the phone away from my ear, but only a little … I didn't want to miss a word.

"And we'd like to invite you to be a contestant—"

I must have been so excited that I squeezed the phone—hard. And because my mom had answered it with her muffin-grease hand, it slipped out of my grasp like a banana from its peel and landed (button-side up) in the muffin batter. My mom gasped.

"—on our show when we film in Gleason next week," Angie Matheson went on loudly, oblivious to the fact that she was now speaking from inside our largest mixing bowl. "Would you like that?"

Obviously, this was a life-changing moment. I didn't have time to worry about washing my hands, or to think about what my mom's coworkers would eat at their coffee break. I reached right in to grab the phone.

"Clara? Are you there?" Angie Matheson asked even louder.

"Oh, yes," I managed finally, bringing the batter-covered phone to my ear. My mom sighed loudly as I picked a raisin out of the bowl with my free hand and nibbled at it nervously.

"Yes, you're there, or yes, you'd like to be a contestant?"

"Two yeses," I answered.

Angie laughed heartily. "Why don't you put your mom back on the phone so I can give her the details about the filming schedule?"

I bit my lip and held the phone toward my mom with an "I'm sorry" shrug. She shook her head and sighed, but there was a small smile underneath it. "I'll help you make more muffins, okay?" I promised. "In a few minutes. I'll be right back."

I had to tell Bradley my news. Right away!

I licked some batter from my hand as I raced across my yard and squeezed through the gap between our fences, accidentally flattening a tulip or two along the way. As usual at that time of day, Bradley was outside digging a hole. He looked up at the sound of my footsteps.

"Bradley!" I said, running toward him. "I just got the best news. I'm going to be on *Smarty Pants*. I got a spot!"

"Really?" He looked up at me. He was smiling, but a smile wasn't the reaction I'd been expecting. A near-deafening shout of joy or at least a double high-five would have been more appropriate.

"What's wrong?" I asked. "Aren't you excited for me?"

"Of course I am," Bradley said, but he hesitated a little. "That's great news." He picked up his trowel and scraped at a big chunk of dirt. "It's just ..." He hesitated. "I got the *worst* news." I could tell he was working up the nerve to say it. "I got a spot on the show too," he said finally.

"Oh." I felt my excitement deflating like a balloon. But to tell the truth, I wasn't 100 percent surprised. Bradley had said he was going to try to do badly at his audition—but he was so smart and so honest that it probably wasn't easy for him to fail on purpose.

"You don't have to worry," Bradley added when he saw how disappointed I looked. "I won't win. I mean, it would be better if you won, so you can finally publish @*Cat*."

I smiled weakly. It was nice of him to say that, but I also knew there were a ton of things he could buy if he had the prize money. He could get some professional equipment for his backyard archaeological digs—or maybe even go on a trip to a real dig site, where they were unearthing dinosaur bones.

"You shouldn't lose on purpose," I told him. "It wouldn't be fair."

Bradley gave a tiny nod. After all, he knew better than anyone that honor and integrity were very important to me—and to @Cat.

THE @CAT CREDO
I am @Cat!
I fight 4 what is right!
I behave with honor & integrity!
I strive to rid the world of k9 evil!
Signed, @Cat

Still, Bradley looked worried—and because I knew him so well, I was pretty sure I knew why.

"Look," I said, "even though you're really nervous, it's going to be great. Now we'll get to meet Mitch O'Toole together. Also, we'll both do our best. Whoever wins wins, right? No matter what, we'll still always be friends."

"Pinky promise?" he said.

I paused. This was super serious. We needed something stronger and more everlasting than a pinky promise.

"How about a spit swear?" I suggested. I spat into my hand and held it out to him.

Bradley made a face. "That's kind of gross. Are you sure?"

In answer, I extended my hand even farther. Bradley was my best friend, and he always would be. I'd never been more sure of anything in my life.

A spit swear is a solemn promise—not to mention a really good way to catch a cold.

Bradley spat in his palm too, then we shook on it. It was official. No matter what happened, I was sure we'd be friends till the end.

Stupid Stinky Party Bus

Bradley and I were as close as ever, but as soon as people got their calls to say they'd made it onto *Smarty Pants*—or had failed to make it on—things started to get ugly at school between other kids.

That Wednesday was a rainy morning, so first recess was indoors. We were finally out in the fresh air for second recess, and Bradley and I were seeing who could hang upside down from the rusty monkey bars the longest. It happened to be a very good position for eavesdropping. For one thing, I had a theory that all the blood rushing to our ears improved our hearing. And for another, it made us look busy even though we weren't doing much. People rarely suspect a person who's hanging upside down.

"It's so unfair," we overheard Becky whine to a bunch of girls.

"Totally," her friend Darla agreed. "You should

get a do-over audition. I mean, it's not your fault you had a semi-serious sprained wrist."

"Exactly," Becky's friend Joanna added. "And if anyone should have *not* got a spot, it should have been me. Like, you're so much smarter than I am, Becky."

This *wasn't* true, but Joanna pretty much had to say it, since she happened to be one of the lucky kids who'd earned a spot. Becky (being Becky) just *had* to be jealous of her friend.

Personally, I was surprised to learn on the bus that morning that Joanna had made it. She was always following Becky around—smirking when Becky smirked, laughing when Becky laughed, and wearing some version of what Becky wore. I guess I'd almost thought of her as *part of Becky*—like the sixth toe on one of those cats that have six toes (which, by the way, are called polydactyl cats). But since I'd found out that Joanna was going to be my competition, I'd started to seriously size her up.

When Mrs. Smith had asked me to borrow some extra science textbooks from Joanna's classroom that morning, I'd taken the opportunity to check out one of her projects on the bulletin board. It was about how the human eye sees different colors, and underneath the perfectly drawn rainbow bubble letters at the top it was marked with an A+. Then, when I passed her desk, I noticed a row of erasers shaped like mushrooms, teddy bears, and kitty cats balanced along one edge. None of them appeared to have been used. A chill ran down my spine. Did that mean Joanna *never* made mistakes?

"Nuh-uh," Darla said, twirling a lock of her hair. "You totally deserve your spot, Joanna. If anyone should have *not* got on, it's him." She pointed across the yard.

Besides Joanna, there were four other contestants from our school. There was me and Bradley, of course, and Abby—which I'd been expecting. Like I said before, she's super smart and strong.

But to my great disappointment, there was also …

"Shane Biggs." Darla made a disgusted scoffing noise after spitting out his name. "Someone please explain to me how the dumbest boy on the planet got a spot!"

Shane was sauntering toward the monkey bars with Jason. Since the second he arrived at the bus stop that morning, he'd been bragging to anyone who'd listen about how the *Smarty Pants* producer had called him first—which he figured meant he'd scored highest in his audition. To make matters worse, he was also planning a big, fancy birthday party that he would *not* shut up about.

Apparently, there would be unlimited pop and pizza, and all the coolest video games. Plus the whole thing was going to happen in a big bus that would be parked in front of Shane's house. Even I had to admit: it *did* sound off-the-charts awesome. Pretty much everyone wanted to go. But he could only invite twenty people.

Shane had been passing out invites that morning, making so much fuss you'd think they were made of solid gold instead of cardboard. As he approached, I could see that he had a stack of them in his hands. They had a shimmery, holographic look to them, and the 3D picture of a game controller on the front seemed so real that I wanted to reach out and touch it. I didn't seem to be the only one who'd noticed it either.

"Stop staring at my party invites," Shane said to Becky as he stomped through a puddle. "You're not coming. None of you are, okay? No girls allowed."

"Oh, puh-lease!" Becky retorted. "Like we'd want to go to your stupid stinky bus party."

"Yeah," Darla agreed. "Especially after what you did to Becky's wrist. It's all your fault she couldn't finish the obstacle course at the auditions."

"Yeah, right," Shane said, sneering. "First of all, everyone knows she's faking that sprained wrist. And second, the reason she didn't get a spot is because she's dumb."

"Just keep telling yourself that, Shane," Joanna replied, defending her friend. "If there'd been any *real* competition for boys' spots, you wouldn't have stood a chance."

I looked over at Bradley, but if he was upset by this remark, it was hard to tell. His face was already red from all the hanging upside down we were doing.

"Oh, yeah?" Shane stepped straight into another puddle to get close to Joanna's face.

"Yeah," Joanna said, giving him a little shove backwards, which caused the party invites he'd been holding to slip from his grasp and land in the puddle.

"Look what you made me do! You are SO dead."
He shoved her back. "And for your information,
I'm going to beat you in the first round."

"Nuh-uh," Becky said. "Joanna's going to win."

Shane smirked. "Joanna's too much of a *girl* to
do the challenges. I heard she wouldn't even touch
a worm in science class because it looked slimy.
She'd never get dirty on purpose."

And *that* was when Joanna surprised even
herself, I think.

"Oh, yeah?" She reached down and picked
up two big handfuls of wet, mucky sand from
underneath the monkey bars. Then she ran toward
Shane and launched them at him.

Time seemed to stand still as a gob of sand-
mush slid down Shane's cheek and landed on the
pavement with a splat. He wiped at his face with
his coat sleeve, then he glared at Joanna.

"Shane!" Jason said. He crouched down, then
held something out to his friend. "Get her back
with this."

It took Joanna a second to realize that Jason had
just handed Shane a fat, juicy worm.

Shane started to fling the worm around so

violently that I worried its body might snap in half.

Joanna shrieked and backed away. "Don't you dare come near me with that, Shane Biggs. Or else!"

"Or else what?" he asked.

"Or else you'll be sorry," Becky said. "You and any other boy who gets in our way."

I sighed. The whole boys-versus-girls fight was starting to remind me a little too much of my latest panels of @*Cat: Doggy Decimator*, and I knew I needed to put a stop to it—if only for the worm's sake.

@CAT
DOGGY DECIMATOR (PART 2)

When we last saw our hero, @Cat, she had just received a video message from the bees. Poodle Noodle and his posse of puppies were peeing on every plant in sight. Somebody had to put a stop to it!

Poodle Noodle! Stop killing those plants!

It was never about killing plants. My posse of puppies and I have peed on every plant in this land, marking them with our scent. According to doggy law, the land of Animalea is now our territory. Ours! Hahaha!

TO BE CONTINUED...

"Bradley," I said urgently. "We need to do something."

As if on cue, we grabbed the monkey bars, swung our feet down, and dropped to the ground in unison.

"Stop it!" I shouted, holding out the palm of my hand like a police officer or an especially angry crossing guard. "If you don't put that worm down right now, I'm telling a teacher."

"Get lost, Clara," Shane said. "This is none of your business."

"Well, I'm making it my business." I struck my fiercest stance—which is kind of a karate-chop pose, but with feet wide apart, like second position in ballet.

"Fine. If you want to make it your business, take this."

Shane screwed his eyes shut, then shook his head from side to side like a wet dog, sending the sand-mush from his hair flying in all directions. Some of it got in my mouth, but I didn't care. I spit it out and focused on what mattered.

"Drop the worm," I said in a firm, commanding voice … and he did. I ran over to check if it was hurt, but it had already slithered into the wet sand.

"Everything all right here?" Mrs. Walsh, the yard monitor, was coming toward us. And because nobody wanted to get detention, we all nodded.

Shane picked up his puddle-soaked party invites, and he and Jason stomped off across the yard, where they immediately started talking to Matteo and Glenn, probably telling them what had happened. Meanwhile, Becky, Darla, and Joanna climbed the monkey bars, where Adila, Siu, and a few other girls met them to get a full report. Every so often, the two groups glared in each other's direction, but there was no more trouble—at least, not that day.

On Set

Smarty Pants aired live on TV—which was part of what made it so exciting. The first taping was right after school on Monday afternoon. There would be eight contestants to begin with—four boys and four girls. Two kids would be eliminated in each episode, leaving two finalists for the finale on Thursday—and one grand-prize winner in the end.

No matter what happened, the days were bound to be action-packed—filled with trials, tribulations, and tons of televised trivia. But while I was thriving under the pressure, I could tell that Bradley was already about to break.

"This is awesome!" I exclaimed as we walked into the front lobby of the building where the show would be filming.

My mom and dad were with me, and Stuart had brought Bradley, as well as his little sister, Val.

To the right was a fancy-looking reception desk

where a secretary sat, and to the left a room with a glass wall. Inside it, there were about thirty TV screens, a bunch of computers, and a big panel with a trillion buttons on it. A man wearing a headset was busy connecting some cables, but when he saw us, he looked up and waved.

"I can't believe we're going to be on live TV in less than an hour!" I said, waving back. "We'll be right on those screens. Broadcast into millions of living rooms across the country!" I knew that Momo and her friend Gerta would be watching us from their retirement home—and that my cousins, aunts, and uncles would be tuning in.

"Aren't you excited, Bradley?" Stuart asked hopefully. When Bradley didn't answer, Stuart gave his shoulder a squeeze. "Just remember the breathing exercises we practiced, okay? And don't forget to keep dreaming big." He added a wink.

When Stuart wasn't looking, I gave Bradley a big cheesy wink of my own, which made him smile. Still, my best friend looked pretty pale.

The receptionist took our names and directed us down a hallway, but we'd taken only a few steps when a little man burst through the last doorway.

"You must be Clara and Bradley," he said, rushing toward us. He had a long, pointy nose and a stooped-over, defeated look about him that reminded me of Dobby the house-elf from the Harry Potter books. He even had the big, worried eyes. In fact, the only thing missing was the puff of smoke he should have appeared in.

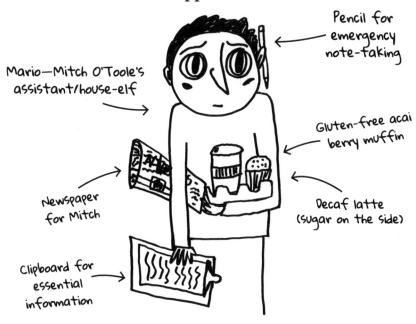

Pencil for emergency note-taking

Mario—Mitch O'Toole's assistant/house-elf

Gluten-free acai berry muffin

Newspaper for Mitch

Decaf latte (sugar on the side)

Clipboard for essential information

"I'm Mario, Mitch O'Toole's assistant. We've been waiting for you. Right this way. Right this way, please. We don't have much time." He showed my parents, Stuart, and Val the way to the audience area.

"Good luck, guys," my mom said.

"We'll be right in the front row," Dad added.

But Mario hardly gave us time to say goodbye. "You'll need to put on your Smart Suits first," he muttered as he hurried down the hall and we tried to keep up. "You'll find the correct sizes waiting in the changerooms with your name tags on them. Then get to makeup. When you're done, I'll bring you to the greenroom—that's where you'll wait for filming to start."

Twenty minutes later, Bradley and I were squished into our super-tight silver Smart Suits, and Veronica, the makeup lady, had coated our faces in thick makeup that matched our skin. It itched like crazy. When Bradley and I were training, he should have mummified me in Saran Wrap to recreate how uncomfortable I'd feel.

Mario came to collect us and we waddled down the hall to the greenroom, which was actually beige. It had big, comfy couches and a foldout card table heaped with snacks. There were crackers (Wheat Yummies—sesame-seed-free!), cheese, cut-up fruit, donut holes, those mini sandwiches without crusts, and so much more. But most importantly, it was where I finally got to scope out the rest of the competition.

Abby was already at the snack table, loading up her plate with an alarming amount of cheese for such a small person. Meanwhile, Shane Biggs was reclining on one of the couches with his feet propped up, staring at his brand-new state-of-the-art cell phone. His mom had bought it for him after the incident in gym class, and (whenever he wasn't talking about his bus party) he'd been bragging about its fifty-megapixel camera and patented anti-glare screen. From the *bleep-bloop–ding* sounds coming from the phone, I guessed he was doing some last-minute studying by answering questions on his Quiz-It app.

"Stop staring at my phone, Clara!" he said when he caught me looking. "For the last time, I'm *not* letting you try it."

I just rolled my eyes and ignored him. Shane acted like I was constantly bugging him, but the truth was, I'd only asked if I could try his Quiz-It app three—or maybe four or five—times in the last few days.

I continued my survey of the room and noticed

that Joanna was sitting as far away from Shane as possible, on the other side of the room, checking her face in one of those tiny folding mirrors. Sitting beside her was a boy I didn't recognize. He had coffee-colored skin and little round glasses that kept sliding down his nose. He was reading a huge book with teeny-tiny print. His name tag said "Lamar." He flipped a page, scanned it super fast, then flipped another. Was he speed-reading?

There was also a girl I didn't know standing near the window. The hood of her Smart Suit was down, and her long, straight hair hung almost to her waist. When she heard us come in, she cast us a sideways glance, then looked us up and down, like she was searching out our weaknesses with her mind.

"Hi," I said, giving her my friendliest smile, but she turned back to the window without a word. Clearly, she was the silent and mysterious type. Either that, or she was just plain rude.

"Do you want a snack?" I asked Bradley.

He nodded, so I led the way across the greenroom. I'd just rounded the sofa when I nearly tripped over a dark-haired boy sitting cross-legged on the floor. His eyes blinked open. "Oh, hello," the boy said serenely.

"Hello," I said back.

"I'm Golden Martinez." He reached a hand up and I shook it kind of awkwardly. "I was just meditating," he said, shaking Bradley's hand next. "It does wonders to increase concentration." Then he closed his eyes and drifted back into his zone. I looked at Bradley and shrugged, then we stepped around the boy to get to the snacks.

But before we'd had a single chocolate-dipped strawberry—

"Oh my goodness!" Abby squeaked. She started hopping up and down. "I just saw him!"

"Saw who?" Bradley asked.

"Mitch O'Toole, of course!" She pointed to the open door of the greenroom. "He went into that room across the hall."

All thoughts of snacks vanished from my mind. I could hardly believe Mitch O'Toole *himself* was mere steps away! And then, as if he didn't want me to wait a second longer to meet him, he emerged from the room, his enormous hair brushing the top of the doorway.

"Hello there," he said as he walked into the greenroom. He extended his hand to Joanna first, then to Shane Biggs and the boy named Lamar. I glanced at his tie, which had—of all things—cats on it! What were the odds?! It had to be a lucky sign.

"Welcome to *Smarty Pants*," he said as he continued making the rounds.

When he got to me and Bradley, I couldn't contain myself. I shook his hand so hard he winced.

"Quite a grip you've got there, Clara," he said.

Mitch O'Toole knew my name! He must have heard all about my stellar audition!

"It's great to meet you," I said, exuding my usual five points of charisma. "I have something for you, actually." I handed him the package I'd brought with me.

"How nice," he said, unwrapping the gift. "It's a waffle tie." He held it up for everyone to see.

"Suck-up," I heard Shane Biggs mutter. But I didn't let it bug me. He was obviously jealous that he hadn't thought to bring Mitch a tie himself.

"Not everyone knows this," I explained to Mitch,

"but Gleason is the waffle capital of the world." It was true. We were in *Guinness World Records* as the town that had hosted the largest-ever waffle dinner.

"Well, how about that," Mitch said. He snapped his fingers and Mario appeared behind him. He got there so fast that I was almost sure I *had* seen a puff of smoke.

"Mario, hang this in my collection," Mitch said, passing the tie over his shoulder. "File it under breakfast foods. And make sure you alphabetize it correctly this time. Waffle. With a *W*. I don't want to find it shoved haphazardly between the bacon tie and the one with mini croissants."

"Yes, sir," Mario said, then he dashed off to do Mitch's bidding.

As soon as he'd gone, Mitch turned his attention to the remaining contestants. "And you must be Golden," he said to the dark-haired boy, who'd broken his meditative trance. "And Tanya." He extended his hand to the mysterious girl with the long, straight hair.

I almost smacked myself on the forehead. Of course! Mitch knew *everyone's* name—because we were all wearing name tags on our silver suits.

"Follow me." He turned on his heel and led the way out of the greenroom.

"Are you guys ready?" Abby asked. She was bobbing around excitedly as we made our way down the hall.

Bradley and I answered at the same time—

And suddenly, there it was in front of us: the *Smarty Pants* set. Only … it was the weirdest thing. How can I explain it?

When I was five or six, I saw a SimpleBake Oven

in a toy catalogue. It looked so shiny, so special, and so state-of-the-art. I *had* to have it. I was going to use its patented baking technology to open my own dessert shop. Finally, after lots of begging, pleading, and letter writing to Santa, I got it for Christmas. I was shaking as I opened the box—I was that excited.

But then I had it in my hands. It was made of flimsy plastic pieces that snapped together. The handle fell off every time you opened the door. The patented baking technology was just a light bulb, and the mini muffins it made tasted like warm Styrofoam.

The set of *Smarty Pants* was like that SimpleBake Oven.

Everything about it looked smaller and less glamorous in real life. For example, the starting blocks that the contestants stand on when the show opens looked like they were made of solid gold on TV, but up close, they were just wooden crates someone had spray-painted. The big backdrop with all its flashing colored lights was a piece of plywood propped up on stilts, and the studio audience area, which had always seemed so vast, was really just fifty or sixty seats lined up on risers.

I looked over at Bradley, wondering if he was thinking the same things, but I couldn't catch his eye. Mario had already shown us to our podiums, and Bradley's was two blocks over. Bradley was staring straight ahead into the bright spotlights.

Just then, the familiar calypso beat of the theme music began. Ready or not (and thankfully I *was* ready), the moment had arrived.

Round One

As round one of *Smarty Pants* began, I tried to focus 100 percent on doing my best, but it wasn't easy.

Things started out well enough.

"Hello, everyone," Mitch O'Toole said, "and welcome to this week's first episode of ..." He leaned toward the audience.

"SMARTY PANTS," they yelled.

"I'm thrilled to be broadcasting from the beautiful city of Gleason today." As Mitch talked, his eyes kept darting off to one side, and that was when I noticed that he was reading off a big screen with scrolling text. It was positioned just past the cameras, out of sight of everyone watching at home. "It's home of the Gleason Cubs Junior League hockey team and—little-known fact," he added, straying from his script, "the waffle capital of the world!"

I grinned.

"I've got eight of Gleason's brainiest fourth-graders with me, and I've got a *feline* it's going to be a *puuuuurfect* day for these kids to match wits." He held up his cat tie.

A woman standing on the sidelines in a red *Smarty Pants* crew T-shirt signaled the audience members with a thumbs-down. They all groaned on cue.

"As always, we'll begin by introducing our contestants. I think today we'll keep it classy. Ladies first …"

At those words, there was a high-pitched shout: "Go, Gleason girls!"

I looked into the audience and saw Bossy Becky with her hands cupped around her mouth.

"Show those boys who's boss!" Darla added.

I guess I should have been encouraged by their cheers, but for some reason, they gave me a bad feeling in the pit of my stomach. Instead of looking at Becky and Darla, I tried to focus on my parents, who were sitting with Stuart and Val, right at the front, where they said they'd be. I also spotted a bunch of kids from school, including Matteo,

Glenn, and Will from my class, as well as Jason.

When Becky and Darla kept shouting out pro-girl slogans, the woman in the red T-shirt frowned at them and made a zip-it motion with her hand.

"Our first contestant is Abby MacDonald," Mitch resumed. "Abby, can you tell us a little about yourself?"

"Sure, Mitch!" Abby rocked back and forth on the balls of her feet excitedly. "I go to R.R. Reginald—but right now we're in the Gledhill Elementary building because of mold. I have two little sisters, and my hobbies include singing, juggling, and building scale models of important cultural landmarks."

It was the classic *Smarty Pants* intro. Contestants almost always gave the name of their school, one fact about their family, and a couple of hobbies. Still, Abby had delivered it with confidence. Plus I'd learned some important information about her—anyone who built scale models of landmarks was bound to know a lot about geography and history. I made a mental note not to underestimate her.

In fact, I knew I shouldn't underestimate anybody. If @Cat were in my position, she'd create a fully searchable Excel spreadsheet of the strengths and weaknesses of every opponent so she wouldn't forget. I wasn't lucky enough to have a keyboard arm like her, but I memorized what everyone said and wrote it down as soon as I got home, along with a few other things I already knew. My spreadsheet looked like this:

ABBY MACDONALD

AKA MOUSE-GIRL

School: R.R. Reginald/Gledhill.

Hobbies: Singing, juggling, building scale models of important cultural landmarks.

Strengths: Straight-A student. Possesses surprising physical strength and willpower!

Weaknesses: Small in size. Easily overexcited.

"It's great to meet you, Abby!" Mitch said. "Next we've got Joanna Schneider. Tell us a bit about yourself, sweetheart."

"Well ..." Joanna tilted her head to one side so she'd look her most adorable, "my name is Joanna. I also go to R.R. Reginald Elementary, which is in Gledhill Elementary right now." She crinkled her nose cutely, like she was trying to remember what came next. "I'm an only child, and my hobbies include figure skating, clarinet, and fashion design."

JOANNA SCHNEIDER

AKA PRETTY KITTY

School: R.R. Reginald/Gledhill.

Hobbies: Figure skating, clarinet, fashion design.

Strengths: Probably has good balance and strong lungs. Strong in science. Rarely (never?) makes mistakes. Fashionable. Possesses powerful cuteness.

Weaknesses: Controlled by Bossy Becky. Easily grossed out by things such as worms.

"Welcome to the show, Joanna," Mitch said.

A loud whistle came from the crowd. "Go, Joanna!" Becky and Darla shouted.

"I see you've got some fans here today," Mitch commented. "And next we've got Tanya Dean."

"Hi, Mitch," said the girl with the piercing gaze and long, straight hair. "I like to study and I play classical piano in my spare time. I just passed level seven. I'm a student at First Avenue Public School."

TANYA DEAN

AKA SAVVY SPHINX

School: First Avenue Public School.

Hobbies: Piano.

Strengths: Bold. Mysterious. Focused. Probably has very fast fingers.

Weaknesses: Could use more charisma.

As Tanya gave her introduction, she stood perfectly straight and didn't smile once. She'd taken a risk by changing up the format for her intro (proving that she was bold), and she'd given less information than most people (making herself mysterious). What she *had* said made it clear that she was smart and confident. My only hope was that because she seemed like such a serious person, it might be hard for her to wade through Jell-O or tie her shoelaces with her teeth.

"And next we've got Clara Humble," Mitch said. "Clara?"

Obviously, I'd had my introduction ready ever since I'd started dreaming of being a contestant. I'd even practiced it in the mirror, just in case the day ever came. But somehow, after hearing all the other speeches, the one I'd prepared felt kind of small and insignificant.

I needed something punchier, spunkier … more memorable.

"Hi, Mitch," I started. "My name's Clara Humble. And the only thing you need to know about me is that I'm unstoppable." I pumped my fist in the air when I said that last part. I was kind of expecting the crowd to go wild—amazed by my boldness. Instead, there was just some polite clapping, which I was pretty sure came mostly from my mom and dad.

"Okay, then," Mitch said. "Fantastic! Let's hear it for the unstoppable Clara Humble!"

The woman in the red shirt cued the crowd and they all cheered, which was a relief. I was starting to feel a little awkward standing there with one fist in the air.

CLARA HUMBLE

AKA @CAT

School: Gledhill Elementary.

Hobbies: Comic book author/cartoonist extraordinaire.

Strengths: UNSTOPPABLE!!!

Weaknesses: Tends to overestimate her own abilities (according to some people, but those people may just be jealous of her many talents).

Then Mitch moved on to the boys—and that was when things started to get a little out of control.

"First up, we've got Shane Biggs," Mitch said.

The boys from my school cheered loudly, and in response, Becky, Darla, and an entire section of girls started to boo.

"Hi, Mitch." Shane had to shout to be heard over all the noise. "My name's Shane Biggs. I just moved from California, where I went to Ferndale School— the best school on earth. But now, unfortunately, I'm at Gledhill Elementary."

SHANE BIGGS

AKA BULL DUHG

School: Gledhill Elementary.

Hobbies: Staring at his phone. Playing video games. Watching TV. Hating everything.

Strengths: Trains with a state-of-the-art trivia app.

Weaknesses: Terrible salsa dancer. Majorly negative *all the time.*

"Go back to California, then!" someone shouted from the audience. I was pretty sure it was Becky.

Shane's face started going kind of red, but he carried on.

"I'm an only child."

"Booooooooo!" went the girls in the audience.

"Yaaaaa!" and "Go, Shane!" answered the boys.

"I like playing Quiz-It on my phone, and also playing video games and watching TV."

The woman in the red T-shirt was doing her best to quiet the kids in the audience, but they refused to be shushed. Finally, after she'd made a few especially angry zip-it motions with her hand and pointed to the door, they settled down. But that didn't stop them from starting up again each time a new boy contestant was introduced. Here's how the rest of them stacked up:

GOLDEN MARTINEZ

OMMM... OMMM

OOOMM...

AKA GOLDEN BOY

School: Carlaw Elementary.

Hobbies: Meditating. Mountain biking. Reading the classics.

Strengths: Focused and centered.

Weaknesses: Unknown.

LAMAR OKPARA

School: Our Lady of Peace Elementary.

Hobbies: Chess. Orienteering. Math.

Strengths: Superior intellect. Reads encyclopedias at super speeds.

Weaknesses: Too serious to complete silly challenges?

AKA CANINE BRAININE

BRADLEY DEGEN

AKA BIJOU THE BRAVE

School: Gledhill Elementary.

Hobbies: Archaeology. Reading comic books (especially *The Adventures of @Cat*).

Strengths: Loyal. Friendly. Smart. Has excellent taste in comic books.

Weaknesses: Sometimes afraid to stand up for himself (for example, the time he let Stuart force him to be on a game show).

Bradley went last. It took him three tries to pronounce the word "archaeology," and he completely forgot to say that he had a little sister, but besides that, it was perfect.

"And now, without further ado," Mitch said, "today's first category is 'Health and Nutrition,' and the topic is 'Marvelous Milk'!"

The curtains behind us parted to reveal eight chairs. In front of each one was a small table with a clear carton of chocolate milk on it. I could already guess that the challenge was going to involve chugging it, and I wasn't the least bit worried.

"Take a seat. And don't forget to put on your safety goggles," Mitch instructed. My chair was first in the row, which meant that I was going to be answering the first question.

"Round one will last a total of four minutes," Mitch explained, "during which time you must drink all the milk in the pitcher in front of you."

It sounded like it was going to be easy, but then he threw us a curve ball.

"Before you go thinking this will be a sipping cinch, there's a *straw-n* possibility things are about to get tricky." All at once, the tables (which were sitting on top of a moving platform), shifted forward until they were about a foot away from us. "You're all about to receive a super-long bendy straw."

Crew members appeared from off-set and started to pass out twisting straws that were as long as my arm.

"If you manage to drink all your chocolate milk through the straw before the buzzer sounds, you'll gain five points," Mitch explained. "But if you get an answer wrong, there's no telling what Daisy the Dairy Cow might have in store for you."

We heard a loud mooing noise and looked up to see a cardboard cutout of a cow attached to a track above our heads.

"Since your mouths will be busy, you'll answer using the keypads in front of you. Any questions?"

Obviously, I had none. (Not to brag, but I'd basically been preparing for this all my life. My mom says that, as a baby, I could suck a bottle of milk down in one minute flat.)

"Great!" Mitch said. "At the sound of the buzzer, start sipping!"

It was harder than it looked to get the milk

flowing, but after the first sip reached my mouth, I was able to keep it coming.

"Clara, you're first! For five points, here's your question. According to the recommendations of dieticians, how many servings of milk and dairy should the average person consume each day? Is it: A—1, B—3, C—5, or D—10?"

We learned the food pyramid in health class every year, so I didn't even hesitate. I pounded the button marked B.

"That's correct," Mitch said.

There was a dinging sound, and my score screen lit up with five points.

"Abby, when you make cheese fondue should the cheese be: A—moldy, B—high in calcium, C—melted, or D—past its best-before date?"

Abby chose C, and Mitch moved down the row. The questions were pretty easy, and everyone got them right until this came along:

"Which one of the following is *not* necessarily found in yogurt? Is it: A—milk, B—bacteria, C—sugar, or D—fat?"

I managed a sideways glance at Bradley. He and I had been best friends forever, so I knew everything about him—including that the tops of his ears turned pink when he was feeling anxious; that he was scared of clowns, saber-toothed tigers, and the dentist (in that order); and that he hated yogurt. What's more, this was the first truly hard question of the day. It also didn't help that Becky, Darla, and several other girls were booing from the stands— just as they'd been doing every time a boy was up.

The seconds ticked by. Finally, he reached for a button.

His answer appeared on the screen: B—bacteria. It was a good guess. You wouldn't think any food would purposely have bacteria in it, but yogurt did. It always had at least a little sugar from the fermentation too. (I knew that from the time my dad was on a diet and read all the labels). What it didn't *necessarily* have was fat.

The buzzer sounded and Daisy the Dairy Cow started to move down the track until she was positioned directly over Bradley's head. He winced, bracing himself for the penalty. I thought for sure that the cardboard cow was going to squirt milk out of her udder and onto his head, but what she had in store was way worse.

The audience gasped as her tail rose and a stream of brown stuff that looked like—well, you can guess—shot out, landing right on Bradley's head. He spluttered as he wiped it off his goggles.

"Ewwwww!" someone shouted.

"Did that cow really just—?" another audience member asked loudly.

"Not to worry," Mitch laughed. "It's only chocolate pudding. Yet another dairy product."

Still, I felt awful for Bradley. Not only was it gross, but getting the first penalty of the game was sure to be a blow to his already shaky confidence. Without breaking the suction on my straw, I tried to turn my head to give him a reassuring look, but I'm not sure if he could see me through the brown smudges covering his goggles.

Summoning all the powers of my cheek muscles, I slurped the last half inch of milk up my straw, then sat back, feeling like I was about to burst. Seconds later, the buzzer sounded and the round ended. Three of the contestants—Shane, Lamar, and Tanya—had a score of only five points because they hadn't finished their milk. Bradley trailed everyone with zero because he hadn't answered his question right or finished the challenge. That meant Abby, Joanna, Golden, and I were tied for the lead with ten points each. But there were still three rounds to go that day, and if I'd learned anything from watching *Smarty Pants* (besides the capital of France, what to call a group of ants, and the name of the most popular cheese worldwide), it was that anything could happen.

Dodecagons
and Deception

Bradley surprised and impressed me that afternoon. Not only did he seem to wipe the chocolate pudding incident from his mind (and his safety goggles), but he let it boost his confidence instead of shaking it. It was as if the worst had already happened, so there was nothing left for him to be afraid of.

He got every answer right and completed every challenge in the rest of the game—which, let me tell you, wasn't easy! The next three rounds were even more fast-paced and skill-testing than the first—and all the booing and cheering from the audience wasn't helping any of us.

After conquering questions on everything from bears to break-dancing, I came out with a perfect score, and so did Abby. Joanna did well too—at thirty-five points—but Lamar and Tanya hadn't done so great. They were strong in trivia, but the challenges were their downfalls—especially in round two (category: literature; topic: *Charlie and the Chocolate Factory*), when we had to sort through a vat of jelly beans with our toes, pick out the reds, and eat them. Tanya kept gagging, and Lamar had terrible toe coordination.

Shane Biggs hadn't done very well either, and it was easy to see why: the girls had booed all the boys—but Shane loudest of all. I was sure he could hardly hear his questions, let alone focus on the challenges. So even though he would still be advancing to the second episode, he wasn't too pleased with his score.

Name	Total
Abby	40
Clara	40
Golden	35
Joanna	35
Bradley	30
Shane	30
Lamar	25
Tanya	25

He stomped off the set into the boys' changeroom—covered from head to toe in honey and glitter from having incorrectly answered a question about bears in round two and landing in a pit of glitter in the disco dance-off in round three. And before he slammed the door so hard that the walls shook, I heard him muttering about stupid girls ruining everything.

Shane was not the type to let something like that go, so looking back, I really should have suspected something the next day on the bus when he dropped his stuff on the seat across from us and went to the back to talk to Jason and some other boys in our class.

"Bradley, look!" I said, pointing to Shane's cell phone, which he'd left on the seat. He usually kept it in the front pocket of his backpack, and I'd seen him check and recheck that it was safe about a dozen times. Unfortunately, none of that was going through my mind that morning.

Despite much begging and pleading, my dad still

hadn't let me download Quiz-It on his cell phone. (It cost $10.99, and I already owed him allowance money from the time I downloaded the I Mustache You app, which lets you put a mustache on any picture you want.)

I glanced toward the back of the bus to make sure Shane wasn't watching.

Bradley could tell what I was thinking. He kind of wrinkled his nose. "I don't know, Clara. If you want to study, why don't you just borrow my book instead?"

He held up his copy of *The Kids' Trusty Trivia Guide* to show me the picture of the giant brain on the cover. Stuart had bought it for him. (Apparently, "Prepare! Prepare! Prepare!" was the fourth Secret to Success.)

"Yeah, but the Quiz-It app's got the world's most complete and up-to-date collection of trivia questions," I pointed out. I'd read all about it in the app store. "Who knows how old your book is!"

Bradley flipped it open to check for a date. "It was published last year," he reported.

"Exactly!" I pointed out. "It's ancient."

Bradley just sighed and went back to his book.

I glanced once more toward the back of the bus. Shane and Jason were sitting behind Will and Roger. They were passing a shiny party invite back and forth. Shane had obviously had more printed.

I couldn't see the harm in borrowing the phone. Especially since I could easily put it back before Shane even realized it was missing.

Quick as a flash, I reached across the aisle. When I switched the phone on, it was already logged in to Quiz-It, and there were several math questions lined up. It was perfect! We hadn't had a math question on day one of the show, so there was a good chance we'd get one on day two. I spent the rest of the ride answering questions about polygons—and getting most of them wrong. But at least I was learning.

In fact, I got so absorbed in trivia that I didn't even notice we'd pulled up in front of the school. Bradley tugged at my sleeve and I glanced back to see Shane walking up the aisle. I switched the screen off and held the phone out to him.

"Your phone ... umm, fell on the floor," I lied. "I picked it up for you, but you should really be more careful with it."

"Oh thanks, Clara," he said, with only the barest trace of a smirk—which should have been another hint.

Then, at first recess, I was sitting on the edge of the sandbox, right where the trunk of the big oak tree splits in two and lets through a shaft of sunlight. Bradley was using the bathroom, so I was flipping through his Stone Age trivia book.

Out of the corner of my eye, I noticed Shane and Jason heading my way.

"What are you staring at, Clara Humble?" Shane asked, flashing one of the hologrammy invites at me. "Don't even ask, okay? No girls allowed at my party."

I tried to go back to Bradley's trivia book, but they wouldn't let me.

"Yeah. No girls," Jason confirmed. Then he stared at my shirt. "Especially not one who dresses like that."

I closed the book and looked down at my sleeve. I was wearing my favorite shirt with sparkly stars on it.

"Yeah. Nice shirt! Those polygons are so irregular," Shane said, looking disgusted.

"*Completely* irregular," Jason agreed.

I pretended to ignore them, but my feelings were hurt. Also, I couldn't help wondering if there really *was* something wrong with my shirt. Finally, Shane and Jason gave up and walked away.

"What did Shane want?" Bradley asked. He'd come back just in time to see the two boys leave.

"Nothing." I sniffed a little. "He just wanted to rub it in that I'm not invited to his stupid party. Also, he called my shirt irregular. Or he said the polygons on it were irregular, anyway."

Bradley laughed, which at first I thought was kind of insensitive. "No they're not!" he said. "Stars are *regular* polygons because all the angles are equal."

That was when I started to wonder …

After recess, during computer lab time, I did a web search and figured out that Bradley wasn't just saying that to make me feel better—it was mathematically correct.

In fact, I let Polly the Polygon from www.math-is-fun.edu.org guide me through a whole unit on geometric shapes, and as she squawked out each answer, I grew more and more certain: Shane's

Quiz-It app was way worse than an out-of-date book! In fact, it was 100 percent wrong—at least when it came to polygons!

"And that could be just the beginning. Maybe his app was wrong about lots of things," I said to Bradley. "Maybe that's why he got so many of his answers wrong in the first round."

I felt pretty lucky that my dad had never let me buy Quiz-It. Otherwise, I might have got my answers wrong too. But that was before I found out that the app had nothing to do with it.

"Mario! Get in here!"

It was day two of the competition. The remaining six contestants—me, Abby, Joanna, Bradley, Shane, and Golden—were once again squeezed into our silver Smart Suits, covered in itchy face makeup, and waiting in the greenroom. Bradley was chowing down on some Wheat Yummies, and I'd already had at least a dozen chocolate-dipped strawberries. I was dying to dig into a big bowl of salt-and-vinegar chips, only I was afraid the crunching would disturb Golden, who was meditating again. Unfortunately for him, though, Mitch O'Toole was in no mood to be quiet.

"Maaaaario!" he called again from his dressing room, much louder this time.

"Yes, sir. Coming, sir." Through the open greenroom door, I saw Mitch's assistant scurry down the hall. "What can I help you with?"

"I can't find my script," Mitch thundered. "I need to review it before the show starts."

"Well, I'm sure I gave it to you yesterday," Mario replied. "Didn't I? At least, it's not in my folder." As if on cue, a folder slipped off the huge stack of papers Mario was carrying and landed on the floor, scattering pages everywhere. As his assistant picked them up, Mitch tapped his foot impatiently, which caused his large hair to bounce from side to side.

"No. It's definitely not here," Mario said finally.

"Well, it's not in my dressing room either. Find it!"

"Right away, sir." Mario scrambled off.

"Wow," said Golden, who had given up on his meditation. "Mitch's chakras could use some serious realigning."

I wasn't completely sure what a chakra was, but I had to agree. *Something* was wrong with Mitch O'Toole. He was all pizzazz and puns when the cameras were rolling, but the rest of the time he was like a different person. Aside from being mean to Mario, he'd shouted at a crew member because the cantaloupe on his personal snack tray was cut into wedges instead of cubes.

"Here you go." Mario came racing back down the hall. "You can use my copy. Five minutes to taping, sir."

Mitch waved the script around in the air like he was shooing an especially pesky fly. "Get lost so I can read this, then."

"Of course, sir." Mario took a step back just before Mitch slammed the door in his face. He stood there for a moment, dabbing at the corners of his eyes. Then he turned, saw us all looking at him, gave his head a shake, and plastered on a smile. "Five minutes to taping, kids. I'll show you to your places."

Mario wished us good luck as he helped us onto our podiums, and a minute later, the lights dimmed and the familiar music began. Once again, Mitch O'Toole bounded in with his mega-big, mega-fake, mega-watt smile.

"Hello!" he said. "And welcome to another episode of ..." He leaned toward the audience members.

"SMARTY PANTS," they yelled.

After the usual introductions, Mitch held up his whale tie. "I just know we're going to have a whale of a time today," he said with a wink. Again, on cue, everyone groaned. "So let's get started. Our first category today is 'Math.'"

I bit nervously at my lip.

"And our topic is …" Mitch paused, waiting for the words to light up on the game board. "'Plenty of Polygons'!" he announced.

I had never been so relieved in all my life. I mean, what were the odds?!

"Your challenge," Mitch said as the curtains parted behind him, "is to ride these bumper cars around the polygon-shaped tracks. Before the buzzer sounds, you must do three complete laps."

The crazy polygon racetrack!

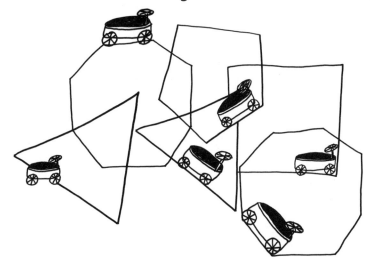

The bumper cars were my favorite ride at the fun fair that came to the Save-o-Rama parking lot every summer, and at first glance, the challenge looked pretty simple.

We each put on helmets and safety goggles and took a seat in the car that had our name on it. Then the starting buzzer sounded and we were off. I stepped on the gas hard.

"Our first question is for Joanna." Mitch had to shout over the buzzing of the bumper cars as we steered them in zigzagged polygon patterns around the tracks. At the first turn, I barely missed banging into Golden, who had managed to pull ahead of me.

"Joanna, a stop sign is shaped like a polygon," he said. "But what type of polygon is it? Is it: A—a hexagon, B—a dodecagon, C—an octagon, or D—a triangle?"

Joanna almost crashed into Abby, but she managed to stop just in time. "A," she called out. "A hexagon."

The buzzer sounded.

"I'm sorry, Joanna, but that is incorrect. Stop signs are shaped like octagons." All of a sudden, her bumper car rose a few inches off the track and started to spin wildly on the spot.

"Ahhhhhhh!" she screamed.

It revolved six or seven times, and then, just as suddenly, came to a stop and crashed back onto the track. To her credit, Joanna didn't waste time worrying about what had happened. She hit the gas right away. But she must have been pretty dizzy, because she crashed into Bradley when his polygon intersected with hers. They both had to back up and decide who would go first, wasting valuable time.

"The next question is for Clara," Mitch said.

I braced myself. Even though I'd learned a lot about polygons in the computer lab that afternoon, math was still my weakest subject. So you can imagine my delight when these words came out of Mitch O'Toole's mouth: "What type of polygon is a star shape? Is it: A—a regular polygon, B—an irregular polygon, C—a five-sided polygon, or D—a pointy polygon?"

"A," I said without hesitating. "A regular polygon." I passed Shane, who had a startled look on his face, and steered right through a tricky intersection.

"That's correct. My next question is for Shane. What is the correct mathematical name for a square that is tilted at an angle? Is it: A—a diamond, B—a side-square, C—a double triangle, or D—a rhombus?"

I'd seen that exact question that morning on Shane's app, along with a completely incorrect answer, and I couldn't help smiling. I would have bet anything (including a pound of real diamonds) that I knew exactly what Shane was going to say, but—

"The answer is D!" Shane announced. "A rhombus."

DING!

"That's correct!" Mitch shouted. "My next question is for Bradley. When we say that a polygon is 'convex,' do we mean ..."

But I didn't listen to all the options, because at that moment a distracting thought popped into my mind. If Shane's app had all the wrong answers (and it did), and he'd studied using the app (which he had), then how was it possible that he'd got that answer right? It didn't make any sense, unless ...

My car collided with Abby's and I felt a sickening

jolt go through me. Shane Biggs had somehow put wrong answers into his Quiz-It app on purpose! And he'd left it on the seat, knowing I'd take it. I'd been sabotaged!

When we last saw @Cat, Poodle Noodle and his posse of puppies had marked all the plants in Animalea with their scent, but that wasn't the end of his evil plan.

TO BE CONTINUED...

Bad Boys

The questions in episode two were tough, and the challenges were tougher. (There's nothing easy about peeling and eating a banana with your teeth while your hands are tied behind your back, but add trivia questions to the mix and it's nearly impossible.) Still, I managed to get a near-perfect score.

The only question I got wrong was in the science category—and it wasn't even my fault! The topic was "Gotta Hand It to You," and the *Smarty Pants* people obviously had some wrong information.

Category: Science
     Topic: Gotta Hand It to You!
Question: How many bones are in
          the human hand? Is it:
               A) 27?
               B) 19?
               C) 105?
               D) 10?

Bradley had spent an entire afternoon on human biology during my training. I knew the answer was definitely nineteen—not twenty-seven, like the *Smarty Pants* people seemed to think! He'd also made me memorize that there are twenty-six bones in a human foot and only three in a human ear—which I guess is why it's so rare to see anyone walking around with an ear cast on. Not to brag, but I was basically a

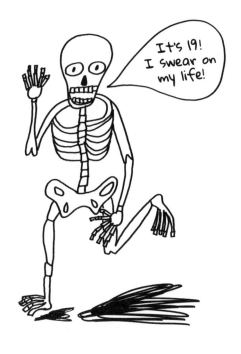

biology expert.

I would have complained to Mario or Mitch O'Toole, but it didn't end up mattering much. I still managed to make it through to the next round.

Name	Total
Bradley	40
Golden	40
Shane	40
Clara	35
Abby	25
Joanna	10

Which was more than I could say for poor Abby and Joanna, who both got booted off the show.

Joanna had got all of her questions wrong and had completed only two of the challenges, leaving her with just ten points. And Abby—usually so quick and clever—had scored a mere twenty-five points. It was so strange. In fact, it was too strange.

"It's not fair," Joanna whined as we started down the hallway toward the changerooms. "I think someone sabotaged me! There was a worksheet about polygons on my desk this morning, and all the answers on it were wrong. Plus," she added, as if something was dawning on her, "at recess, Shane and Jason kept talking about how you can make salad out of the leaves of rhubarb plants, when the truth is that they're poisonous. So I got my nutrition question wrong too." She turned to glare at Shane, who was walking behind us with the other boys.

"Wait a sec!" Abby stopped and put her hands on her hips. "Is that why you and Jason were talking so loudly about potassium-rich fruit and vegetables on the bus?"

Shane smirked.

"I knew that didn't seem like a normal conversation for nine-year-old boys!" she said.

"Not so fast!" I reached out and grabbed Shane by the shoulder as he tried to push past us. "*And* you left your phone on the seat for me to take, and your app had all the wrong answers."

"Okay, first of all," Shane said with an infuriating smile. "None of you have any proof that I did anything. And second of all, last time I checked, there weren't any laws against leaving a piece of paper on someone's desk. Or against having completely innocent conversations about fruit and vegetables. It's not my fault that you were eavesdropping. And it's definitely not my fault that you stole my cell phone this morning."

Before any of us could get a word in edgewise, Shane stalked down the hallway and into the boys' changeroom.

"Can you *believe that*?" I said to the other kids.

"Oh, there's *no* way he's getting away with this!" Joanna was almost in tears.

Abby was fuming too. I could tell by how red her face was as she followed Joanna into the girls' changeroom.

I turned to see how Golden and Bradley were reacting to the news, but just then—

"MAAAAARIO!" Mitch O'Toole came storming down the hall. "Get out of my way," he said to us.

Bradley and Golden had to flatten themselves against one wall, and I ducked into the changeroom to avoid getting mowed down.

"Where is my after-show mango smoothie?" I heard Mitch shout at his assistant. "I'm parched!"

Inside the girls' changeroom, the mood was heavy. Joanna and Abby had already started unzipping their Smart Suits for the last time. They looked totally dejected—and angry.

"But what I don't get," Abby was saying, "is how Shane knew who would get which questions today. It doesn't make any sense."

"First you lose my script," we heard Mitch yell at Mario, "and now my smoothie is late! What do I pay you for, anyway?"

I think we all realized it at the same time.

"Of course!" I said.

"The script!" Abby exclaimed.

"He stole it. That good-for-nothing, sneaky, horrible, stupid, stinky Shane Biggs," Joanna hissed.

"Right from under Mario's nose," I added. It was bad enough that Joanna and Abby were off the show, but the fact that Mario was getting yelled at for something Shane did was so unfair.

"And that's not all," Abby said. "Did you notice that all the boys got perfect scores today—not just Shane?"

I *had* noticed, of course—but that couldn't have anything to do with Shane stealing the script, could it?

"You think he gave *all* the boys the answers?" I said. "That can't be true. I mean, Bradley would never cheat!" My best friend was so honest that he'd once insisted we knock on a neighbor's door and return a nickel we found near the end of her driveway.

"Well, maybe not Bradley," Abby agreed. "But Shane could have given the answers to Golden if he really wanted to eliminate the girls from the competition. And you know how much he hates girls."

"First he pushes Becky over in gym class, then he tries to throw that disgusting worm at me, and now this!" Joanna said. "Well, I'm not putting up with it!" She did up the last button on her shirt, then threw her Smart Suit (still covered in mashed bananas from round two) into the hamper. "I'm telling my dad!"

With that, she marched out the door. And just five minutes later …

"I want to see Mitch O'Toole this second!" It was a man's voice—deep and demanding—coming from the hallway.

Abby and I walked closer to the open changeroom door to hear.

"Now, sir. If you have a complaint, it's important to go through the proper channels." That was Mario. "I have a form here that you can fill out." We could hear the rustling of papers.

"I'm not interested in a form!" answered the man.

"Daaaaadddy. Do something!" Joanna whined. "That's his dressing room. Right there."

By then, Abby and I had positioned ourselves so we could peek out into the hallway.

Joanna's father—a big, broad-shouldered man in an important-looking business suit—was already standing in front of Mitch's door, banging on it with his fist.

"Yes?" Mitch O'Toole opened the door. He sounded impatient, but it was hard to tell for sure because we couldn't see his face. The hulking figure of Joanna's father filled the doorway.

"My daughter was sabotaged, and I want to know what you're going to do about it!" Joanna's father boomed. "Some boy—"

"Shane Biggs," Joanna supplied.

"That's right. Shane Biggs gave my little girl all the wrong answers. How did he know what questions were going to be asked today? What kind of ramshackle operation are you running that would see a contestant getting access to that information?"

Mario was waving his hands frantically now, trying to soothe Joanna's dad, who was getting more furious by the second.

"I don't think—" he started. "If we could all just take a step back and calm down, I really believe that—"

"Now see here," Mitch O'Toole interrupted. "I will not have you trespassing backstage, making crazy accusations. If your daughter had known the answers to the questions, she wouldn't have lost the game. Mario!" Mitch snapped his fingers, and Mario scooted around Joanna's father and into the room. "Call security and have this man escorted out."

"That won't be necessary," Joanna's dad said. "But you *will* be hearing from my lawyer." He took Joanna by the hand and stormed off down the hall.

As soon as they were out of earshot, Mitch hissed at Mario, "You! Get in here immediately. I want to talk to you about that missing script."

Mario whimpered softly, but he followed Mitch into the dressing room. The door slammed.

Once we were alone, Abby and I stepped out into the hallway. She looked down miserably at her *Smarty Pants* name tag, which she was holding in her hand. I didn't blame her for being upset. It was the only souvenir she'd get to keep after losing her place on the show. And a crummy old name tag was worse than nothing when you compared it with the thousand-dollar prize. It would have been different if she'd lost on her own, but to have Shane sabotage her was so unfair!

Just then, the door of the boys' changeroom

opened and the villain himself sauntered out. He was busy talking to Golden and didn't notice us there at first. "Yeah," he was saying, "it's next Friday. You should come." Shane handed him one of the party invites. "Back in California, my friend Ian had a video-game bus party once, and it was insane. People here usually have such lame birthday parties. Trust me, you don't want to miss mine."

That was when I realized that Abby might have been right! If Shane was giving one of his oh-so-precious party invites to Golden …

"Yeah. Sounds cool," Golden said. "I'd love to come." Then he gave Shane a fist bump. "Peace out. See you tomorrow."

… and if they were on a fist-bumping-basis, then that meant they *must* be friends. And if they were friends, there was a good chance Shane had given Golden the answers just to get the girls off the show!

It was bad enough that Shane was out to get us, but now I was sure that Golden was in on it too!

Abby seemed to be thinking exactly what I was thinking.

"We can't let them get away with this," she said.
And it turned out that she and I weren't the only ones who felt that way.

Plotting and Planning

The next morning before the bell rang, Abby came to find me and Bradley.

"Everyone's talking about how Shane stole the script," she reported, sitting down beside us on the edge of the sandbox. "I heard Becky say Joanna's dad might even sue the show to see if she can get back on. And Becky and her friends are planning something major to get revenge."

Now, I'd be the first to admit that since Shane, Jason, and Golden were determined to play dirty, *someone* had to do *something* to stop them, but much like @Cat, I usually preferred a peaceful solution to problems. Revenge wasn't really my scene. And even if it were, Bossy Becky was the last person I'd want to work with.

"Maybe we should go and find out what Becky and the girls have got in mind," Abby suggested.

"I don't know …" I said. I glanced across the

yard to where Becky had rallied a group of girls. They were pacing around the monkey bars as they (presumably) plotted and planned. Joining forces with an enemy was an extreme move.

But then again, after what Shane and his friends had done, had they left us much choice?

"What do *you* think, Bradley?" I asked.

"Huh?" He clearly hadn't heard a word we'd said. His nose was buried in *A Hundred Brain Boosters for Boys*, the latest book Stuart expected him to read.

"About Becky," I said. "Should we go and find out what she's doing to get back at Shane and his friends?"

When I'd met Bradley in the parking lot after the show the day before and told him about the stolen script, he'd seemed even more shocked and outraged than I was—but he wasn't Becky's biggest fan either. I was counting on him to weigh in on the problem, so I was more than a little surprised by his response.

"Uh," he said absently. "Yeah, I guess."

I gave him a puzzled look.

"I mean, yeah. We should do that," he said more definitely.

And that was when things took a sharp and sudden turn for the terrible.

As he started to stand up, Bradley slid a piece of flimsy cardboard out of the back of his book and used it to mark his page.

It happened fast—almost too fast to be seen by the human eye. But I have incredible eyesight (almost like a raptor, hawk, or other bird of prey), so it wasn't fast enough. I would have recognized the shiny holographic card anywhere.

The invite of ultimate betrayal!

"What's that?" I asked, narrowing my eyes at the thin edge that was sticking out of the book.

"Huh? What? Nothing." Bradley pushed it down out of sight, but the second our eyes met, he knew that I knew he was lying.

I had a moment of almost dizzying disorientation as a million questions raced through my mind: Had I really just seen what I thought I'd seen? Did it mean what I thought it meant? It couldn't. *Could it?*

I grabbed Abby's arm and started to pull her up. "We'll be right back," I said to Bradley. I needed to catch my breath and sort things out, and a second opinion couldn't hurt.

"Wait? What just happened?" Abby said as I pulled her across the yard toward the picnic benches, where we'd have some privacy. "Are we going to talk to Becky now? Why isn't Bradley coming?"

I told her about the party invite I'd just glimpsed.

"You don't *really* think …" she started. "I mean, Bradley would never work with Shane to sabotage you. He's been your best friend your entire life. And anyway, just because Bradley's been invited to Shane's bus party, that doesn't mean he's going."

I raised my eyebrows. "Maybe not," I said. "But then why was he trying to hide the invitation in his book? He could have just told me about it."

Abby couldn't think of a good response to that. And before we could discuss it anymore, the bell rang.

I kept hoping I was wrong about Bradley and the party invite, but as the morning went on, there was no denying it: he was definitely acting weird.

Whenever Mrs. Smith gave us independent work time in math, Bradley would always pretend he needed to sharpen his pencil, then drop a note on my desk on his way past. But that morning, no note.

Then, at 10:15, when the fourth-grade girls were going to health class in gym A and the boys were going to health class in gym B, Bradley walked past me without so much as a secret handshake!

I lost track of him on the way out to first recess, but I was determined to find him. I was planning to ask outright if Shane was trying to turn him against me. But Bradley wasn't at our usual spot at the picnic tables, or digging for archaeological treasures in the sand pit—or even at the wall ball wall. In fact, I couldn't find him anywhere.

I met Abby near the picnic tables and told her everything I'd been thinking.

"First of all," I said, "when we found out we both got spots on *Smarty Pants*, Bradley said it would be better if I won. But suddenly, he's super competitive. Don't you think that's weird?"

"A little," she agreed. "I mean, he studies all the time. Every spare second."

"Exactly!" I said. "And he says Stuart is making him, but—"

"It's not like Stuart is looking over his shoulder on the bus, forcing him to study," Abby interrupted, completing my thought.

And there was something that had been nagging at me: that wrong answer about the number of bones in the human hand. Had Bradley purposely misled me in my training? I mentioned it to Abby, and she nodded gravely.

"If we can't be 100 percent sure he's with us," she said, "then it's safest to assume he's against us."

She was right: all the signs were pointing to my worst fears being true, and it would be foolish to ignore them.

"Clara, look!" The big flower decoration on Abby's hat wobbled as she motioned with her head.

I looked over my shoulder. By the playground equipment, a group of boys had congregated. Standing right at the top of the slide on the big jungle gym was none other than Shane Biggs—looking like a king in his castle. He was leading his followers in some kind of a chant.

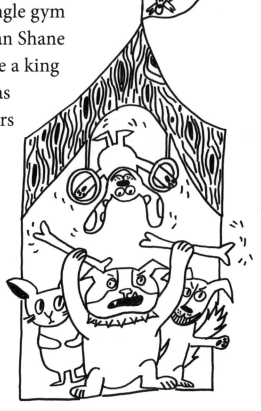

"What are they saying?" Abby asked.

"I don't know," I answered. It was hard to hear, but it was getting louder by the second.

On Shane's left, I wasn't surprised to see Jason, and behind Jason stood Aiden Jackson, who had a reputation for being sneaky and underhanded. (Nobody had forgotten the time he'd dumped out all the jelly beans in the "guess how many jelly beans" jar at the school BBQ and counted them behind the bouncy castle.) Will and Roger were also nearby. And Glenn was dangling from the fire pole. But then I noticed someone else climbing up the ladder and coming to stand beside Shane.

It was Bradley! He was putting one hand on Shane's shoulder and leaning in like they were old friends.

I felt my heart sink. If I'd had any remaining doubts about Bradley's lack of loyalty to me, they'd just been smashed to smithereens.

"Are you okay, Clara?" Abby asked.

"Yeah," I said. I bit hard at my lip to keep from crying.

I took a deep breath and turned away from the boys on the climber—including my best friend. I knew now what I needed to do.

"Come on," I said, and together, Abby and I

walked toward the monkey bars, where Becky was gathered with her group of girls.

"What do *you* want, Clara Humble?" she said, giving me her usual "too busy to be bothered with you" look. But then I explained that we wanted to help.

"Clara has more of a stake in this than anyone," Aimee said, "since she's the last girl left on *Smarty Pants* after the sabotage."

Becky seemed to consider this, and then her whole attitude toward me changed. She tossed her curly blonde hair over her shoulder and put her hands on her hips in a way that made it clear she meant no nonsense.

"There's no way we can let the boys get away with this," she said.

"You're right," I said. For once—weirdly enough—I couldn't have agreed with Bossy Becky more.

"In fact," she shouted, raising her hands in the air, "I declare an all-out war!"

Joanna, Darla, Angela, Aimee, and a few other girls cheered, and even Abby gave a mouse-like squeak of approval.

"The boys versus the girls!" Becky announced.

All the girls roared again—all the girls except me.

"And for our first battle," Becky continued, "we're going to make sure that Clara Humble, the last girl on *Smarty Pants*, wins that show. Whatever it takes!"

As Becky talked she climbed up the monkey bars so that her voice would carry farther. All around the yard, girls and boys were turning to see what was going on.

"And when Clara wins *Smarty Pants*," Becky went on, "it's going to be a victory for every girl—and a defeat for all the boys!"

At that, the girls went completely nuts again.

Meanwhile, I stood under the monkey bars, nibbling nervously at my fingernails. Did I want to win *Smarty Pants*? Of course I did. Comic book fame and fortune awaited!

But could I really join an all-out war against the boys when my very best friend happened to be one?

I looked across the yard to where Bradley was standing on the climber. He still had one hand on Shane's shoulder, only now his lips were moving too. Was he chanting in time with the rest of the boys? It was getting louder, and now we could hear the words clearly, carrying across the yard:

"Boys are best! Boys are best! Boys are best!"

Then again … if my best friend was working against me, he couldn't really be my best friend, could he?

When we last saw @Cat, she was trapped under Bull Duhg's net. Thankfully, Bijou the Brave arrives to save the day. But wait! Things are not what they seem . . .

And that was why, when Becky proposed her big plan to take the boys down a notch, I raised my hand to vote that we go ahead. I even volunteered to be the group secretary and wrote down our battle plan in the little notepad I had in my back pocket.

When we were finished, Becky pumped one fist in the air and asked: "Are you ready to fight hard and *win*?"

All the girls cheered again—and this time, I joined in.

Snug Suits

Bradley avoided me the rest of that day at school. And he must have asked his nanny to pick him up, because he wasn't on the bus home. In fact, it wasn't until my mom had parked the car in the *Smarty Pants* parking lot and we were headed toward the doors that he made an appearance. He was with Stuart, his mom, and his little sister in the bananamobile.

"Hi, Clara!" he called out the window, all innocent-like, as they drove past. I clenched my hands into fists. After plotting with Shane and the boys, he had some nerve pretending to be friendly!

"Clara!" he called again after they'd pulled into a parking spot and he'd slammed the car door shut behind him. "Wait up!"

I did *not* wait up.

"Clara," my mom said, "Bradley's calling you."

"Can't talk now," I muttered. "Need to focus."

My mom shook her head in bewilderment. She probably would have lectured me about the importance of putting friends first, but just then, her cell phone rang.

"It's a video call from Momo," she said, handing me the phone.

"Hey, Brat!" Momo said. "All ready for today's show?" The rest of the way across the parking lot, she and I tried to guess what the challenges might be and planned which board games we'd play when she got to my house the next day. She'd already promised to come watch me in person if I made it to the last round—and I was positive that I would.

"Clara!" My mom tapped me on the shoulder. "Look!"

We'd just crossed the reception area, and she was motioning toward the doors behind us. "It seems like Clara's got a few fans here today," Mom told Momo, laughing. I tilted the phone so that Momo would be able to see for herself. *A few* was an understatement! There were tons of girls pouring through the doors, most of them carrying signs with my name on them.

A herd of girls (aka cats) and one mouse.

I scanned the pack, looking for Abby, and finally spotted the red flower on her floppy sun hat. She noticed me and gave a thumbs-up. It was our signal. The plan the girls had made in the schoolyard was about to go ahead.

Out of the corner of my eye, I saw her break away from the crowd and, quick as a flash, dart down the long hallway and toward the performers' door. She used the *Smarty Pants* name tag she'd been allowed to keep to gain backstage access while the rest of the group veered left through the doors for the studio audience. Abby was stealthy—not to mention brave.

Luckily for us, there seemed to be lots of chaos in the studio that day—which helped our sneaky moves go undetected.

As I started down the hallway to the changerooms, I came within inches of being run over by a frenzied crew member with a messy ponytail.

"Where's the extra-large vat of instant chocolate pudding?" she shouted as she ran past. "It's twenty minutes to taping. We need it NOW!"

"We ordered vanilla pudding for this episode," I heard another worker answer. "I already dyed it green. Today's script specifically said *green* slime."

It turned out that pretty much all the "slime" used on *Smarty Pants* for the different challenges was made of some sort of pudding. It was a relief in some ways (especially when you got some in your mouth by accident), but a letdown in others.

"No! It's brown pudding today. BROWN! We need chocolate, not vanilla," the crew member with the ponytail wailed. "Mario!" She ran up to Mitch's assistant, who was pacing in the hallway and looking even more worried than usual. "We have a pudding situation."

"Oh, dear," he said, shuffling through his ever-present stack of papers. "We can't have a pudding situation. If there's just one more mistake, Mitch will never forgive me."

"Excuse me, Mario," another crew member interrupted. "Is Mitch ready for hair and makeup yet?"

"I'll find out in just a minute," Mario said. "Let me deal with this pudding problem, then I'll be right with you."

I saw a flash of movement by the door of the boys' changeroom. Abby's hat flower disappeared around the corner, but not before her thumb stuck up in a signal: mission accomplished.

"Mario!" Mitch boomed. The host threw open his dressing room door and walked out holding a strip of shiny fabric at arm's length. "Does this look like a toucan tie to you?" He shoved the tie so close to Mario's face that the assistant took a step back.

"No, s-s-ir," Mario stammered. "I believe those are macaws."

"They're *cockatoos*! But that's not the point! I need to wear my toucan tie today. If I don't wear my toucan tie, my opening pun won't make sense. And yet this"—he thrust the tie in Mario's face again—

"is what I found waiting on my dressing room table."

"I'm sorry, sir," Mario said, scurrying into Mitch's dressing room. "It was a careless mistake."

I shook my head. I wished there was something I could do for poor Mario, but at that moment, I had bigger problems. I looked up and saw Shane, Bradley, and Golden walking down the hall toward their changeroom.

Shane said something, and both Bradley and Golden laughed—which was bad enough— but then Shane put his arm around Bradley's shoulder. I ducked into the girls' changeroom and pressed against the wall, feeling like the air had just been knocked out of me.

"You're the best, Bradley," I heard Shane say as they passed. Bradley said something back that I couldn't quite make out. There was more laughter.

Were they talking about Shane's upcoming birthday party? Plotting more sabotage? Making fun of me? I didn't know, but I couldn't afford to let it upset me. I had a show to win.

"Hello, everyone, and welcome to another episode of …"

"SMARTY PANTS!"

When the theme music played that day, I felt strong, smart, and sassy—but underneath it all, I also felt a touch guilty—especially because I couldn't help noticing how Golden, who was standing on the podium next to mine, was shifting around uncomfortably.

"That's right, it's *Smarty Pants*," Mitch trumpeted, "the show where fourth-graders battle it out for the right to call themselves the smartest kid in their city. I'm here today in beautiful Gleason with four of the area's cleverest kids. Starting on the left, I've got Clara Humble from Gledhill Elementary."

Of course, I felt a little better when I looked out over the studio audience and saw it packed with girls. When Mitch said my name, they went wild: whistling, cheering, and screaming like I was a rock star.

"Right beside her, we've got Golden Martinez from Carlaw Elementary," Mitch announced.

A few kids from Golden's school cheered, but they were drowned out almost immediately by the booing of the girls. Golden tried to wave to his friends, but he couldn't quite manage it. He glanced down at his arm, puzzled.

"Also from Gledhill Elementary, we've got Bradley Degen and, last but not least, Shane Biggs."

"Go, boys, go!" a chant started up in the crowd. I looked out and saw that Jason was leading a chorus of boys. Still, they had nothing on the girls in terms of numbers.

"Booooooooo!" the girls answered loudly.

The crew member in charge of the audience was waving her arms and making frantic shushing motions, but it wasn't doing any good.

Finally, Mitch O'Toole just had to shout over the noise. "Today—" he started, but he got drowned out. "TODAY," he tried again, "is the semifinal round. That means tomorrow we'll decide our winner. So, kids," he said, still yelling, "you're going to want to *gopher* it and give it your best."

He held up his tie, which had pictures of gophers

on it. Mario must have failed to find the toucan tie, which explained why I'd seen him walk out of Mitch's dressing room with his head hung low.

"Our first category today is 'The Natural World,' and the topic is"—Mitch motioned toward the screen and the words lit up—"'Remarkable Rain'!"

I breathed a sigh of relief. Once again, I'd been spared a math question.

The velvet curtains behind us parted to reveal four extremely large flowerpots with our names written on them.

"We all know that rain makes the flowers grow," Mitch said, leading us over. "So put on your petals and hop into your pots."

Mario and three crew members emerged with ridiculous flower-petal hats for each of us, as well as the usual safety goggles.

They showed us the stepladders attached to the side of each pot.

"Well, that's unpleasant," Golden said, wrinkling his nose after he'd climbed his ladder and peered into his pot.

That was putting it mildly. The pots were filled nearly to the brim with the usual pudding/slime (this time a swampy green color), but sprinkled on top was a bunch of brown chunky stuff. I guessed this was Mario's quick fix to make the green pudding look more like soil. Whatever it was, it looked nasty.

I shrugged, swung my leg over the top of the pot, and dropped into the muck. It spilled over the sides and made a sucking sound as I sunk in, but I didn't mind. If all that was standing between me and the grand prize was some chunky pudding, it was hardly a match.

Once I was inside my pot, I glanced over to check how the boys were doing. Bradley had just started to lower himself down into the goop, but

Shane was struggling to lift his arms up high enough to reach the top of his flowerpot, and Golden couldn't seem to swing his leg over at all. Finally, some workers had to give Shane and Golden boosts to get them in.

Meanwhile, I looked out into the audience, locked eyes with Abby, and gave her a thumbs-up.

The Girls' Ingenious Plan to Beat the Boys

Step 1: Abby uses old name tag to gain backstage access. Slips into boys' changeroom undetected.

Step 2: She locates stash of extra-small Smart Suits.

Step 3: Abby replaces boys' usual Smart Suits with smaller suits. Sneaks out, again undetected.

Step 4: Boys unknowingly squeeze into too-small suits, making them a little clumsier and a lot more squished.

Step 5: Clara gains an edge. Makes it to semifinals. Goes on to win $1,000!

Step 6: Clara becomes award-winning comic book author. @Cat merchandise is sold in airport gift shops worldwide!

"Your challenge," Mitch explained, "will be to climb out of those pots before the buzzer sounds. But wait," he went on, "there's something missing here."

From somewhere in the rafters above us, four cardboard clouds descended.

"There are our rain clouds now!" Mitch laughed.

The buzzer sounded to start the round.

"Shane, you're up first. How fast do raindrops typically fall? Is it: A—100 to 200 miles per hour, B—7 to 18 miles per hour, C—1 to 2 miles per hour, or D—70 to 80 miles per hour?"

The seconds ticked by, and finally, Shane made a guess. "B," he said over the booing of the girls. "Seven to eighteen miles per hour."

DING! "That is correct," Mitch said. He turned to Bradley next. "What shape are raindrops? Are they: A—teardrops, B—squares, C—triangles, or D—spheres or hamburger buns?"

A few people in the audience actually laughed at that question. It did seem way too easy. But sometimes on *Smarty Pants*, the easiest-seeming questions were actually the hardest.

By then Bradley had freed both his arms from

the muck and was trying to push against the sides of his pot, but with no luck.

"Booooooooo!" all the girls called.

He slipped back down with a squish, then re-emerged, wiping guck off his safety goggles.

"A," he shouted. "Raindrops are teardrop-shaped."

It definitely seemed like the right answer. They were always shaped that way in cartoons. But ... *BZZZZZT!*

"I'm sorry, Bradley," Mitch said. "Little-known fact, but the correct answer is D. Smaller raindrops are actually shaped like spheres, while larger ones take on the shape of hamburger buns. Oh, Sinister Storm Cloud, what penalty do you have in store for Bradley?"

The was a rumbling of thunder from the sound-effects booth, and then the cardboard cutout cloud above Bradley's head started to shake. Suddenly, with a huge gush, it began to pour water. Bradley threw his hands up over his head in a futile attempt to stay dry.

Seconds later, the simulated rain stopped. All in all, the penalty wouldn't have been that bad, except for the fact that the pudding in his flowerpot was now watered down, making it even more slippery.

I didn't have time to watch what Bradley would do next, though. I'd just managed to wedge the soles of my feet against the sides of my own pot. A few more inches and I'd be able to throw most of my weight over the side.

"Clara," Mitch said.

I held tight to the sides of the pot, unwilling to lose focus now.

"Which continent gets the least precipitation? Is it: A—Antarctica, B—North America, C—Australia/Oceania, or D—Europe?"

"A," I shouted with confidence, even though I was only about 60 percent sure. "Antarctica."

DING!

"That's correct!" Mitch said.

I gave myself one last push and, with a squish and a slurp, pulled my body from the pot and hopped to the floor. All the girls in the crowd went insane. I waved one mucky hand at them, then bowed humbly before glancing back at the boys. Golden looked like he was about to cry with frustration, and Shane seemed to have a mouthful of pudding. But Bradley, despite the super-slippery watered-down goo—*SQUELCH! SQUISH! POP!*— managed to emerge, swinging his legs over the side and landing on the floor with a plop.

All the boys in the audience started jumping around and high-fiving each other. Bradley looked over and grinned at me. Was he rubbing it in? Trying to shake my focus? I couldn't let it get to me. I had three more rounds to go to make it to the finals, and there was no way I was letting anyone— least of all Bradley—get in my way.

The Semifinal Round

Our second category was History. The topic: Ingenious Inventions. For our challenge, we had to build a working robot out of various wires, plastic blocks, and power supplies. And even though I got my trivia question wrong (who would have guessed that Play-Doh was originally invented to be a wallpaper cleaner?) and my table started shaking so hard that my robot almost fell apart, I still managed to construct a working bot before the timer went off. So did Bradley.

Third up was Arts and Culture. The topic: Halloween Around the World. The stage crew

wrapped us each from head to toe in about ten rolls of toilet paper to make us look like mummies, and we had to break free.

Shane and Golden both showed a total lack of knowledge about the origins of witchcraft and jack-o'-lanterns, and it took them an extra-long time to get out of their mummy wraps—partly because of their snug suits, and in Shane's case, partly because he kept shouting insults back at the girls and wasn't really focusing.

But the really bad part for Shane and Golden came in the Nutrition and Health category. The topic was Oooooooom: Yoga for Relaxation. We had to copy crazy yoga poses while answering questions about the ancient form of exercise. Normally, Golden would have been a natural, but when he did a cat pose, one of the seams of his suit burst at the shoulder. And when Shane attempted downward dog, his suit split in a very unfortunate spot, and the whole audience saw his lucky underpants!

Then Shane got hit with a penalty when he didn't know which of the following was not a type of yoga: Hatha, Kundalini, Ashtanga, or Tortellini.

A crew member came out and replaced his yoga mat with one that was covered in Vaseline. Bradley got a penalty too, but he still managed to do a perfect thirty-second stork stand without slipping. He must have summoned some serious Zen, because I could barely do it *without* Vaseline on my mat!

By the time the last round ended, we were all covered in green pudding. The only difference was that while Shane and Golden were grumbling and pulling at their ripped Smart Suits, and I was rubbing a bruise on my cheek from a yogic face-plant, Bradley was—somehow—still smiling.

Name	Total
Bradley	35
Clara	35
Shane	15
Golden	10

When Mitch took one of my hands and one of Bradley's and declared us destined for the finals, I smiled, pumped my fist in the air, and waved to the girls like the confident victor I knew they needed me to be. But inside, I was feeling more than a little worried. If Bradley could tie with me despite the too-small Smart Suit, I knew I was definitely going to have to step up my game. And that was before I realized that he was an even fiercer opponent than I'd bargained for.

I was in the greenroom having some post-show snacks when I saw Shane and Golden standing outside Mitch's dressing room door. They were arguing in whispers.

"You do it," Shane said. "He likes you better."

"Are you kidding?" Golden whispered back. "He doesn't like *anyone*!"

"Well, *someone* has to tell him."

Finally, Golden worked up the courage to knock.

"What?" Mitch snapped, sticking his head out the door. He had some kind of mud face mask on and didn't seem pleased to have been disturbed.

"Um, sorry to bother you," Golden started, "but we thought you should know that we put on the wrong Smart Suits today. They were extra-small."

"Well, that wasn't very bright, was it?" Mitch shot back, already closing the door.

"But"—Shane held his hand flat against the door to push it back open—"it wasn't our fault! They were left out for us on the tables. Where our suits always are. With our name tags on them."

"It's true," Golden confirmed. "Both of ours were the wrong sizes. Bradley's was too at first, but he noticed in time and changed into the right size. He tried to warn us, but we were already on set."

So that explained how Bradley had managed to breeze through the episode. It figured that he'd check the size before putting his suit on! His awesome attention to detail was practically superhuman. How had I forgotten to factor that in when considering his strengths and weaknesses?

"It's completely unfair," Shane whined. "We'd still be on the show if it wasn't for those suits!"

"Even if your suits were too small," Mitch said, staring the boys down, "it doesn't change the fact that you both got most of your questions wrong. Now"—he started to pull the door closed again— "get out of my sight before I call security."

I loaded up a cracker with three pieces of marble cheese and bit into it as I watched Shane and Golden stand, dismayed, in front of the closed door. I might have felt sorry for them, but it totally served them right for sabotaging the girls. Finally, Golden took a deep, calming breath, shrugged, and walked off down the hall. But Shane didn't handle the situation nearly so gracefully.

"Uuuugh!" he screamed. "This is so unfair!" Then he stomped around for a bit before finally storming off.

A moment later, Mitch opened the door again. He was gritting his teeth. "First the stolen script, then he's late with my smoothie and my toucan tie goes missing, and now this costume nonsense!" He took a huge breath, filling his lungs. "MAAARRRRRIIIOOOO!" he bellowed so loudly that a crew member walking past dropped the armload of dirty safety goggles she'd been carrying.

"Yes, sir?" Mario popped out of a nearby doorway as if he'd been lingering there, waiting to be summoned.

"YOU'RE FIRED!" Mitch screamed. Then he

slammed his dressing room door so hard that the walls shook.

For a moment, Mario just stood there, clutching his stack of papers to his chest like a life preserver. "But …" he started. "I …" He paused. "Sir," he said with a pitiful squeak. And then Mario did something you almost never see grown-up men (even ones who look like elves) do in public: he started to cry. Big, fat tears slipped down his cheeks one after the other, landing on his folders.

I couldn't just stand by and watch. First of all, the missing script was Shane's fault—not Mario's! But if I'd known that Mario was going to get blamed, I never would have agreed to Becky's suit-switching plan! I gulped down my cracker, stepped out into the hallway and around Mario, and started to bang on Mitch O'Toole's door.

I was going to tell him everything. I'd say whatever I needed to say to get Mario his job back and turn this whole thing around, even if it meant getting grounded for life or—I gulped at the thought—kicked off the show. Things had clearly gone too far, but …

"My decision," came Mitch's voice, muffled by the

door but still plenty loud, "is FINAL!"

I stood there for a moment. Should I try again? I knew I should, but when I turned to look, it seemed like it was already too late. Mario was halfway down the hall. I watched as he passed off his armload of folders to a startled crew member, wiped at his eyes with his sleeve, and ran out the studio doors.

The Day of the Bathroom Blockade

The next day marked a new and ugly chapter in the war between the boys and the girls. Not surprisingly, word got out about what the girls had done to the boys' Smart Suits, and a thirst for revenge was in the air.

"You're going down for this, Clara!" Shane snarled at the bus stop. Because I was the last girl on the show, he blamed me, even though all the girls had been in on it. In fact, a lot of the boys blamed me especially … but I wasn't their only target.

On the bus ride, Will and Roger—who were sitting in the seat behind Adila—put her long ponytail out the bus window and then closed it. When it became clear that the window was stuck, she started screaming. The driver had to pull over to deal with the incident. There were forms to fill out and everything.

That made the whole bus late for school, and the girls were *not* impressed. In fact, while we were all waiting in the office to get our late slips, Adila's friends Aimee and Siu shoved Will and Roger into the giant lost-and-found bin, which always smells like a combination of sweaty socks, sour milk, and that lunch meat with the bits of macaroni in it. The girls got in trouble, but that didn't stop Siu from trying to trip Roger on his way out of the office.

Then Shane Biggs, Jason, and a bunch of other boys retaliated by organizing a bathroom blockade. Basically, it meant that all day long, they kept trying different ways to keep us out of the girls' bathroom—from taping the door shut with a roll of masking tape they found in the photocopier room to smearing white glue all over the door handle so we wouldn't want to touch it. They didn't even stop when Principal Demerit caught Jason posting a fake Out of Order sign on the door and gave him a week of detention. In fact, it only seemed to make the boys more determined.

"That's what you get for making us smell like the lost and found," I heard Will tell Siu after she'd gone into the bathroom and come right back out again, having discovering that all the toilet paper was missing.

At recess, somebody drew a line in chalk down the middle of the paved section of the yard. The boys started shouting at any girl who set foot on their side, and the girls did the same.

Mrs. Smith said we were driving her crazy, and Principals Franco and Demerit made a joint announcement to say that anyone caught taping a door or hiding toilet paper would be sent straight to the office. But nothing seemed to help the situation.

As for me and Bradley, we kept our distance. He sat beside Shane on the bus, his nose buried deep in a trivia book, and he stayed on the boys' side of the schoolyard at both recesses. Meanwhile, I was surrounded by girls at all times, but that didn't stop him from throwing a murderous glance or two my way.

"So?" Becky said, when we were gathered under the rusty

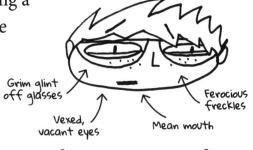

Grim glint off glasses

Vexed, vacant eyes

Ferocious freckles

Mean mouth

Bradley's murderous face.

monkey bars at second recess. "What's the plan for helping Clara win the last show?"

"Well, we're definitely going to make extra signs," Joanna started. "And do *lots* of booing."

I sighed. Don't get me wrong—it was a start. But when Poodle Noodle and his evil twin, Poodle Doodle, attacked the land of Animalea, did @Cat hold up a sign?

Heck no! She fought for what was right and outwitted them at every turn. When needed, she even fired up her billion-megawatt processor and used its powerful rays to melt her enemies into piles of gooey rubber!

"Maybe we should give Bradley false facts, like the boys did to the girls in round two," a girl called Penny suggested, a little more helpfully.

"But how?" Darla asked. "The boys have got him surrounded."

It was true. Bradley was sitting at the top of the jungle gym, studying a trivia book, and the boys were standing guard on all sides.

"Even if we *could* give him false facts," Siu pointed out, "how would we know what the questions were going to be? We don't have a script."

There was a murmur of agreement.

"Well, maybe we can distract him somehow," another girl offered.

"We could put itching powder in his underpants," Tiffany Jones suggested.

"But how are we going to get his underpants?" a girl with two braids asked.

"Okay, then, what about his socks?" Tiffany suggested. "It's really hard to think clearly when you have itchy feet."

But it turned out that nobody knew where to get itching powder—or if it was even a real thing.

"Wait a second," Abby squeaked. "I've got it! We

steal his glasses. Think about it: if he can't see what he's doing, he can't win."

It was an interesting thought, but Bradley was as blind as a bat (or more accurately, as blind as a blind mole rat, since technically most bats aren't blind). What if he tripped and fell and really hurt himself? As much as I wanted to win, I wasn't sure I'd be able to sabotage him like that.

I was just about to suggest that we think of something a little less devious when a shower of gravel came raining down upon us.

"Take that!" Roger said as he ran past, tossing handfuls of the stuff. Shane Biggs wasn't far behind him, and before long, boys were running past the monkey bars, launching an attack.

"Eat dirt, Clara Humble!" Will yelled as he climbed up on the monkey bars and dropped a handful of gravel right on my head.

"Everyone! Protect Clara!" Becky called out, and a human shield of girls started to form around me. At about that time, Mrs. Walsh, the yard monitor, noticed what was going on and called for backup. She and another teacher started yelling at the boys to stop immediately and go straight to the office, but the boys were so wound up that none of them paid any attention.

And it was as I huddled in the middle of the girls, listening to all the commotion, that I realized this thing was bigger than me and Bradley. It was bigger than *Smarty Pants* too. In fact, the battle between the sexes had been going on for ages. Not between me and Bradley, of course, but all around us.

Sure, *Smarty Pants* had taken things to a whole new level—and Shane's bragging about his boys-only party hadn't helped—but most girls had quietly stopped inviting boys to their birthdays in second grade. And even back in kindergarten, the boys always hogged the blocks, and some of the girls told Matthew Okah he wasn't supposed to wear the frilly apron and bake imagination muffins in the pretend kitchen.

Heck! For all I knew, maybe the feud reached back even farther! Did boys and girls gang up on each other in the park as babies? Did they make faces at each other from their cribs in the hospital just after they were born? I couldn't remember, but it was possible that the battle between boys and girls was as ancient as the feud between cats and dogs.

Everyone knows cats and dogs hate each other, but why?
Could the feud date back to the days of
the cave-dogs and cave-cats?

Maybe, I thought as the yard monitors shouted at Shane, Jason, and Will and pointed toward the door, boys and girls weren't even *supposed* to be friends! Maybe it was coded into our DNA!

And now the girls were counting on me to win *Smarty Pants* and settle the score once and for all. But was I willing to do whatever it took?

As the boys stomped off toward the office and the protective circle of girls around me began to break up, I looked over at Bradley. He hadn't taken part in the gravel war—but that was probably because he didn't want to get his hands dirty.

Instead, he'd been sitting at the top of the play structure, ignoring my plight while he read yet another trivia book. Three boys stood around him on lookout. When he got to an especially hard-to-remember fact, he wrinkled his nose in concentration, just as he always did.

I swallowed hard and made up my mind. I knew I couldn't let my heart get in the way. Somehow, I had to win this thing.

My mom and dad picked me up after school and we went straight to the train station to get Momo. She was waiting by the benches with her polka-dot wheely suitcase, and I ran over to her the second I saw her.

"Ooooh!" she said, squeezing me tight in her arms. "There's my girl."

Since Momo had moved, I'd visited her at the retirement community a bunch of times, but this was the first time in almost six months that she'd been back to see us.

She hugged both my parents, then my dad grabbed her suitcase and we started for the car. As we walked, she asked my parents about the new gardening store in our neighborhood, and they asked her about the handbell choir she was in, so it wasn't until we were in the car that Momo and I really had a chance to talk.

"So?" she said, leaning in close. "With all this competition going on, how are things between you and Bradley?"

That was Momo for you. She liked to "cut to the chase," which is an old-person way of saying she's never embarrassed to ask the hard questions right away.

"Good," I lied. But Momo cleared her throat in a way that made it obvious she didn't believe me. "Okay, not good," I admitted. "We're kind of having a fight."

I could tell that my parents were listening from the front seat, and I knew that they'd been worried about me and Bradley too. My mom had asked more than once if everything was okay. But it had been a crazy couple of days since the show started filming. There hadn't been much time to talk. My dad turned up the volume on the radio to give us a little privacy.

"I'm sorry to hear that," Momo said, then she

stayed really quiet for a while. It's one of her tricks. Sometimes she tries to fool you into figuring things out for yourself. I didn't mean to fall for it, but long silences make my brain jumpy.

"It's not like I *wanted* to fight with him," I said finally. "It just happened."

"Mmm-hmmm."

"Because we're competing against each other now, and only one of us can win, right?"

"I suppose that's true," she said.

Momo and I used to play cards three or four times a week when she lived next door. She didn't like to lose, and she never let me win just because I was a kid. She understood about competition. We were both quiet for a minute, then she reached over and slipped something into my hand—two somethings, actually.

"Shiny pennies. For good luck," she said with a wink. "One for you, and one to give to Bradley."

I didn't see how we could *both* be lucky—there was only one thousand-dollar prize—but I took both the copper coins anyway and tucked them into my pocket with a small sigh.

Open Sesame!

When I got to the studio, I could tell that the boys had already been hard at work. The first thing I found was a banana peel right in front of the girls' changeroom door. Like *that* wasn't the oldest trick in the book! I picked it up and went inside, only to discover my Smart Suit laid out for me on the chair, when it was usually on the table. I checked the label.

Nice try, guys, I thought as I flung the extra-small Smart Suit aside and went to get the right one from the closet. When I opened it, I found a big note taped to the inside of the door. Scrawled in marker, it read: "You suk, Humble. You will never winn!"

Boys! They have no subtlety. Also, some of them can't spell. I ripped it off and threw it in the recycling bin. Honestly, I was disappointed by their lack of initiative. I could also tell by the sloppy delivery that Bradley hadn't had a thing to do with those pranks—but that didn't mean he wasn't plotting something else. On my way into the studio, I'd seen him high-fiving Shane Biggs in the lobby.

Just as I finished getting into my properly fitting Smart Suit, I heard a slight rustling of paper. It was a note being slipped under the door.

Clara Humble
Girls' Changeroom
Gleason Public Television Building, Studio 3
3 Halton Road, Gleason

Thursday, May 12

Clara,
Please meet me at the snack table in the greenroom in fifteen minutes.
I need to warn you about something!!!

—Bradley

It was definitely Bradley's handwriting. The spelling was perfect, and he'd even used correct letter-writing format. This couldn't be the work of Shane or the other boys. I paused and considered my options. How could I be sure that if I showed up in the greenroom, no one would be waiting behind the door to trip me, smash a pie into my face, or worse? I dropped the note into the recycling bin as well.

There was no way I was going to go, unless …

A thought crept into my brain. I could get there first and catch *Bradley* by surprise. I pinned my name tag onto my Smart Suit and ducked out the door, glancing both ways to make sure that the boys' changeroom door was still closed.

"Hello?" I called out, poking my head into the greenroom. Nobody answered, so I tiptoed in. Except for the cushy couches and tables filled with snack trays, the room was empty. I glanced at the clock on the wall. If Bradley was coming to play a trick on me, he probably wouldn't arrive for another ten minutes. I had time for a quick snack—something to fortify me for the challenges that lay ahead.

I reached for a cracker, then stopped cold.

There was a box of Wheat Yummies sitting innocently enough on the table right next to the cheese platter. I picked up one of the crackers and nibbled

193

it. Yup. It was subtle, but it had a definite sesame taste. Bradley was going to be devastated when he found out he couldn't eat his favorite crackers anymore!

Mario used to be in charge of the snack table. He knew the allergies and food sensitivities of every contestant, but now that he was gone, someone must have forgotten about Bradley's oral allergy. And *that* was when it occurred to me: here was my opportunity to put my cleverness and cunning to use to score a victory for girls everywhere, make a cool thousand bucks, and achieve comic book fame all at the same time!

After escaping Bull Duhg's net and the clutches of his evil twin, Poodle Doodle, @Cat knew she had to fight back—for the sake of the land of Animalea!

By triggering Bradley's tongue itch, I might be able to give myself the edge I needed. After all, it wasn't like the boys had been playing fair. Plus it was just an itchy tongue. I wasn't going to deflate him like Poodle Doodle!

I snatched the cracker box off the table and tossed it into the nearby recycling bin, covering it with some papers. Then I grabbed a few crackers and shoved them into my mouth before stealing out of the greenroom like a thief in the night— only, you know, in the daytime, wearing a shiny silver suit, and with a mouth full of crackers.

Once I was back out in the hall, it became clear that the snack trays weren't all that was suffering. Without Mario around to keep the details straight, things were a disaster backstage. Workers were running back and forth with large pieces of cardboard, a woman with a clipboard was shouting into her cell phone about a late pudding delivery, and I could hear the boys and the girls in the studio audience trying to out-chant each other.

I sat in the changeroom for at least ten minutes, waiting for someone to come get me, but nobody did. Finally there was a frantic knock on my door.

"Where have you been?" a crew member yelled when I opened it. "You should be on your podium by now."

I bent down and tucked Momo's lucky pennies into one of my socks, then I followed the crew member as she ran toward the set. I took my place behind the curtains and Bradley came in a moment later, just as breathlessly.

"Clara! Did you get my note?" he whispered.

"Oh, I got it," I said, but I refused to look at him.

"Why didn't you come to the greenroom, then? I was waiting for you."

"Of course you were waiting," I said. "That's *exactly* why I didn't come. I'm not dumb, Bradley. I knew you were probably planning to smush a pie in my face."

Bradley sounded confused and also a little disappointed. "There was pie?" he said. "I didn't see any pie."

"One minute to showtime, kids," said a crew member as he ran past with an armload of plastic bats.

"The reason I wanted to meet was to warn you,"

Bradley whispered again. "It's about the boys. They're planning to—"

"Stop," I said, holding up one hand. "You're only going to lie to me again, and I really don't want to hear it."

"Lie to you?" Bradley squinted at me. "What are you talking about?"

But just then, the music started, the lights came on, and Mitch O'Toole bounded onto the stage.

"Hello!" he shouted, plastering on his made-for-TV smile. "And welcome to another episode of—"

As always, Mitch leaned out toward the audience with one hand cupped around his ear—but this time, two things happened: first, I saw a whole bunch of boys in the audience bend down and reach into their backpacks; and second, Bradley yelled, "Duuuuuuck!"

Using my quick-as-a-cat reflexes, I jumped off my podium and took cover behind it, just avoiding the half dozen or so ripe tomatoes that were headed my way.

Some of them sailed through the air, right past the space where I was supposed to be standing …

… but others collided, splattering and squashing into Mitch O'Toole and his giant hair.

My heart was racing, and I peered out nervously from behind my podium, expecting Mitch to explode into a fit of rage but, of course, the cameras were rolling.

"Oh, HAHAHA!" Mitch said instead, wiping some tomato seeds from his tie. "I see we have some jokers here today." The cameras cut to the audience, and Mitch used the opportunity to signal one of his crew members to deal with the situation.

He moved on, barely missing a beat. "I'm here in beautiful Gleason for this week's finale of *Smarty Pants*." He scraped tomato seeds off his shoulder with the back of his hand. "That's right! One of these lucky kids—Clara Humble or Bradley Degen, both from Gledhill Elementary—will walk away today one thousand dollars richer!"

The crowd went wild—with all the girls chanting my name and all the boys chanting Bradley's.

"I can see that our studio audience members are rooting, or should I say 'ruta-baging'"—he held up his tie of the day—"for their favorite contestant."

This time nobody even needed a reminder to groan.

"So let's get the game started." He picked a glob of mushy tomato out of his hair and dropped it onto the stage. "In this final episode, each contestant will answer two questions in each category and there will be just three rounds of play. Our first category is 'Math.' And the topic is"—Mitch looked toward the scoreboard—"'Fun with Fractions'!"

I felt like I might faint. Besides long division, fractions were my worst mathematical enemy.

"This will be a true-or-false round," Mitch explained as the curtains parted and he led us to our places. There were two chairs set up with a divider between them. In front of each chair was a table with a checkered tablecloth. From the sidelines, two workers came out carrying pizza boxes.

"Have a seat," Mitch said, "and put on your safety goggles."

Once we'd taken our places, a worker opened the box in front of me to reveal a large pepperoni pizza.

So it was going to be an eat-off!

"When the buzzer sounds," Mitch said, "begin eating, but remember"—he raised one finger ominously in the air—"there's no need to be piggies. You'll find a pizza cutter in front of you. For today's challenge, you must each eat exactly sixteen-thirty-seconds of the delicious pizza pie in front of you."

The fraction lit up on the question board like something out of my worst nightmares. But before I even had a chance to panic, the buzzer went and the round began.

"Clara," Mitch said. "True or false? Twelve over twenty-four and twenty-four over forty-eight are equivalent fractions."

"Ummmm ..." I had just picked up my pizza cutter. I needed to eat sixteen-thirty-seconds of the pizza. That meant I should slice my pizza into thirty-two equal pieces and eat sixteen of them. Feeling like a pizza genius, I ran the cutter right down the middle to make a first cut while I considered the question. Was twelve over twenty-four equivalent to twenty-four over forty-eight? How was I supposed to know?

"True," I said, taking a guess.

"That's correct!" Mitch said.

I breathed a sigh of relief and made another cut in my pizza, then two more, until I had eight equal slices.

"Bradley," Mitch said. "True or false? Four over nine and twenty-eight over sixty-three are equivalent fractions."

"Too," Bradley said—but what he really meant was "true." Was my plan already starting to work? Had he eaten a sesame cracker? Or was his mouth just full of pizza? I couldn't tell.

DING!

"That's correct!"

"Clara," Mitch said. "True or false? Five over four and five over twenty-five have a common denominator."

I remembered Mrs. Smith writing something about common and uncommon denominators on the board a few months earlier, but at exactly the same moment, I'd been busy working on a panel for a comic called @*Cat vs. Poodle Noodle: Project Doggenator*, so I hadn't been completely paying attention.

In desperation, I took another wild guess.
"False!" I said.

DING!

"That is correct," Mitch answered.

I didn't even hear what Bradley's next question
was. I had cut my pizza into thirty-two slices, but
they were a long way from even. There was also
tomato sauce everywhere, and all the pepperoni
was falling off. I glanced at the countdown clock:
less than thirty seconds to go. I grabbed a handful

of slices and started to mash them into my mouth, but before I could even swallow, the timer for the end of the round sounded.

"Ooooooh," Mitch said as the camera zoomed in on my face and the mess that used to be my pizza, which was mostly clenched in my fists. "It doesn't look like you managed to eat sixteen-thirty-seconds of that pizza, Clara. And, Bradley, you ate exactly half."

I smiled smugly as pepperonis fell from my mouth. I may not have completed the challenge and scored five extra points, but at least Bradley hadn't either!

"Which is equivalent to sixteen-thirty-seconds when reduced to its simplest form!" Mitch shouted.

What? I choked down the last of the pizza in my mouth as Bradley's scoreboard lit up with a total of fifteen points to my ten.

Clearly, drawing @Cat cartoons in math class wasn't the best idea I'd ever had.

The curtains closed so the crew could prepare for the next challenge, and Mitch O'Toole told everyone to sit tight because we'd be riiiiiight back.

As soon as the cameras stopped rolling, he

grabbed a crew member by the sleeve. "I want to know which of those little brats threw tomatoes at me," he yelled.

A team of people emerged and went to work, picking seeds out of his hair.

Meanwhile, Bradley and I walked back to our podiums to prepare for the second round. To avoid having to look at my former best friend, I bent down and pretended to retie my shoelace.

"I was trying to warn you about the tomatoes," Bradley said with a sigh. "Shane Biggs and some of the boys were planning it all day. That's why I wanted to meet you in the greenroom."

"*Just* Shane and some of the boys?" I asked pointedly, looking up at him. Then I stood up so we'd be face to face. "You expect me to believe that?"

Bradley gave me a puzzled look. "Well, yeah."

"Oh, please, Bradley. Don't insult my intelligence and *don't* lie to me."

"I didn't," he said. His eyes had gone big and round behind his glasses. "I mean, I would *never* lie to you."

I glared at him with the hatred of a thousand

honey badgers—which (despite their adorable name) are some of the angriest animals on earth.

Finally, he had the decency to look down at the floor. "Okay," he said in a small voice. "I did lie to you about one thing: Stuart didn't *exactly* force me to audition for the show. I mean, it was his idea at first, because he saw how, when it comes to you and me, you're always the one in the spotlight and I'm always the one helping you. He said I needed to 'Go for gold.'"

I rolled my eyes at the mere mention of Stuart's fifth Secret to Success. First of all, what Bradley did was none of Stuart's business. And second of all, of course I was always the one in the spotlight. Bradley hated being the center of attention!

"When we saw the announcement for the auditions on TV, you just assumed that you'd be trying out and I'd be the one helping you."

I bit my lip. *Had* I assumed that? Well, maybe I had. But only because I knew Bradley so well.

"You didn't even ask if I wanted to try out too. Even though I usually know as many answers as you do."

Now that he mentioned it, Bradley *did* know

most of the answers—he just didn't shout them out as loudly as I did, or get as upset with the contestants when they got something really easy wrong.

"So you're right," he continued. "I lied to you. I just didn't know how to tell you that I wanted to be on the show too. Because I knew how much you wanted to win." He blinked his big, sad-Bradley eyes at me from behind his glasses. "Do you forgive me?"

I put my hands on my hips and stared him down. "Nice confession," I said. "But honestly, I pretty much knew that already. I mean, you've been studying like crazy. I could *maybe* forgive you for lying to me about wanting to try out. But that isn't what I meant. I was talking about how you're working with the boys to sabotage me!"

"What?!" Bradley cried.

"Oh, don't pretend you don't know what I mean," I spat. "For starters, you gave me that wrong answer about the number of bones in the human hand. And I saw you chanting with Shane on the jungle gym." I was gearing up to make my biggest and most indisputable point. "Plus you're going to

Shane Biggs's boys-only birthday party—or at least, you got invited. So you're probably going because you're practically best friends with him now! I see you together all the time."

"First of all, I didn't give you a wrong answer," Bradley countered. "If I'd had that question, I would have got it wrong too. The book we were using must not have included the eight wristbones in the answer. And I wasn't chanting. I was telling them to stop!" He frowned, then he leaned forward accusingly. "And anyway, so what if I'm with Shane sometimes? I see you with Becky and the girls all the time!"

For a few seconds we stared each other down, both with our arms crossed firmly.

"Look …" Bradley rubbed at his forehead in frustration. "You're *still* my best friend. I'm just trying to be nice to Shane. And the only reason I didn't tell you about the party invite was because I knew you'd be mad."

"Of course I'm mad!" I yelled. "How can you possibly be nice to Shane or go to his party after all the mean things he's been doing to me and the other girls?"

For a second, Bradley looked flustered. "Remember what he said that day in gym class? That if he won the show, he'd use his prize money to buy a ticket home to California?"

"Yeah," I said. "And that's the one bad thing about him not winning. He'd be packing his bags soon!"

"But don't you think that's sad? Of all the things in the world he could spend a thousand dollars on, all he wanted was to leave Gleason. He hates it here that much."

"Uh, that fact is pretty hard to miss," I said. "He talks about it constantly."

"And nobody at our school likes him much either," Bradley went on. "I heard a bunch of the boys say they're only hanging out with him because they want to go to his video-game party. Even Jason said so."

"Oh," I said. And even though Shane was still one of the worst people on earth, learning that information did make me feel just a little sorry for him. Jason was *supposed* to be his best friend.

"I just thought that if someone was actually nice to him, maybe he wouldn't be so miserable here anymore," Bradley explained. "And then he might even stop acting like such a jerk. And anyway, he *is* our new neighbor. Just because you don't like him doesn't mean I can't try to be friends with him, does it?"

Well, of course that's what it means! That's exactly what it means! I wanted to shout. But as the words were en route from my brain to my mouth, I realized how wrong they sounded. Bradley and I had always been best friends, but that didn't mean I had the right to tell him who he could and couldn't spend time with.

"Okay, but how come you've been ignoring me?" I asked. My voice caught in my throat when I said it. The truth was, that part had really hurt my feelings.

"I wasn't ignoring you!" Bradley said. "I was studying. Anyway, I figured you were probably busy studying too."

I looked at the scoreboard—which showed that I was five points behind Bradley. I *should* have been busy studying. Instead, I'd been spending a lot of my time worrying, plotting, and planning. And if this was all really true—if Bradley really was still my friend—then …

"Huh. That's weird." Bradley scrunched up his face, then he opened his mouth and tried to scratch his tongue with his teeth.

The Wheat Yummies crackers—*Now with Sesame!* They were starting to take effect! What had I done?

The Grand Finale

"Places, everyone! Places!" Mitch O'Toole yelled. "Thirty seconds."

The commercial break was ending, and Bradley and I had to step back onto our podiums.

"Welcome back," Mitch O'Toole said. "We're here in beautiful Gleason with Clara Humble and Bradley Degen, who are battling it out for the right to call themselves the smartest kid in the city. It's time for our second category, 'The Natural World.' And the topic is 'Cave Dwellers.'"

The curtains parted, revealing a huge, gray cardboard ... something.

"As you answer this round's questions," Mitch explained, "you'll make your way through this creepy cave maze on your hands and knees, with only the lights on your helmets to show you what lies ahead. Here in the studio audience and at home, we'll follow your progress thanks to the handy cameras attached to your helmets, and you'll hear your questions and give your answers through these neato headsets."

I looked at the cave nervously. Not many people know this about me, but although I am almost completely brave and fearless, the one thing that scares me, just a little, is small, dark places. I think it goes back to the time I was playing Harry Potter and accidentally locked myself in the broom closet.

The entrance to the pretend cave was narrow and led into a pitch-black tunnel. What if my headlamp burned out and I got lost in there and never came out the other side?

"It's okay," Bradley whispered when he noticed the terror in my eyes. Then he made another weird face while he tried to scratch his tongue against the roof of his mouth. "We'll stick together, okay? Just follow the sound of my voice. We'll find our way through."

I nodded, gulped, and took my place at the mouth of the cave.

The buzzer sounded and I followed Bradley in. Almost immediately, I heard Mitch's voice in my ear.

"Clara," he said as Bradley took a right turn and

I followed, "there's a special name for species like millipedes, blind salamanders, and eyeless fish that live in caves in perpetual darkness. Are they called: A—cave dwellers, B—dark dwellers, C—troglobites, or D—underground animals?"

Thankfully, Bradley and I had learned about those kinds of animals in the bat cave at the Science Center. "C," I said. "Troglobites." Then we came to another intersection in the maze. Bradley looked to me, and I nodded toward the right.

Me and Bradley in the bat cave at the Science center.

DING!

"That's correct!" Mitch said.

As we listened to the next questions, we crawled forward in the cave and took another right and two more lefts. Bradley looked back over his shoulder every now and then to make sure I was directly behind him.

"Bradley, what is spelunking? Is it: A—using echoes to find objects in a dark space, B—exploring caves, C—dropping stones into the water in caves, or D—spelling in caves?"

"The answer ib B, Mitch. Explobing caves," Bradley said. His tongue was clearly starting to get itchier, but I was relieved that it hadn't stopped him from answering. That one was easy, after all—well, for us, anyway. The summer before, we'd gone on a camping trip and my dad had taken us spelunking—which turned out to be less funny than it sounded.

The time Bradley and I went spelunking.

"Clara," Mitch said, "a stalagmite is a type of crystal that grows upward from the surface of a cave. But what is the name of a crystal that grows downward? Is it: A—a dropping crystal, B—an amethyst, C—a stalactite, or D—a saltine?"

I knew that one too! In second grade, Bradley and I were crazy about rocks. We both had huge collections.

Me and Bradley, rocking out in second grade.

Bradley took another left, then waited to make sure I followed.

"C," I answered, "stalactites." And then I breathed a small sigh of relief because I could see a light at the end of the tunnel up ahead.

"Bradley," Mitch said, "for the final question of

the round: Are bats: A—birds, B—flying reptiles, C—mammals and birds, or D—mammals?"

"Duh," Bradley said.

"What's that?" Mitch asked. "I couldn't quite make out that answer, Bradley."

"I bed d-uh," Bradley repeated. He'd definitely eaten more than one cracker! Maybe even lots more.

"Bradley, would you like me to repeat the question?" Mitch said through our headsets.

But I knew he didn't need the question repeated. Bradley knew bats were mammals. We'd done a project in third-grade science. He also knew that they can catch up to twelve hundred mosquitoes in an hour, and that they sleep hanging upside down so they can launch themselves into the air to escape predators. But Bradley couldn't tell Mitch any of that—let alone answer the question—because his itchy tongue was out of control.

"Time's running out, Bradley," Mitch said. "Do you have an answer for us?"

"I bed duh," he tried again, but it all sounded like gibberish.

"He's saying D," I said into my headset. "The answer is D."

The buzzer sounded.

"I'm sorry, Bradley, but the rules state that you must give your answer yourself."

Suddenly, there was a flurry of fake bats filling the cave—which must have been the penalty—but we were so close to the exit that it didn't really matter. We just pushed our way through them and came out the other side into the light, completing the challenge.

As Mitch announced the commercial break, I tried to breathe. I felt sweaty and shaky, and I knew it wasn't just my claustrophobia (trivia fact: that's a fear of small spaces).

"Bradley!" I said, grabbing the sleeve of his Smart Suit. "Is your tongue going crazy?"

"Yed!" he said. Then he stuck his tongue out and scratched it with his fingernail.

"The crackers in the greenroom ... they had sesame in them," I said with a little yelp. "I saw the box, but I put it in the recycling bin because I was so mad at you. I was hoping it would give me an edge."

Bradley looked confused but not mad. Not really.

"And that's not the only bad thing I did," I

confessed. "I plotted with the girls to switch all the boys' Smart Suits to the little ones, including yours—only you noticed in time."

"*Dou* did dat?" Bradley said in dismay.

"Well, technically Abby did it and it was Becky's idea, but I voted for the plan," I explained.

He shook his head. "Clara, why would dou do dat?"

I shrugged helplessly. *Because I was too competitive for my own good? Because I wasn't as nice a person as Bradley? Because I had a bad habit of not really thinking things through?* I thought all that, but all I said was "I'm sorry."

Over the years, we'd had our share of problems. One time, Bradley refused to sleep over at my house because I said that we had to watch *My Little Pony*, and that I got to have the comfiest chair, and that we were putting extra butter on the popcorn (even though Bradley said it made the popcorn soggy). And another time, when we were playing *Dragon Quest* and my dragon killed his dragon ten times straight, he got so tired of my bragging that he tossed his controller onto the couch. But I'd never—not once—seen Bradley do what he did next.

Without a word, he turned his back on me and walked away.

"Wait!" I cried. "Bradley!" But he just kept going. He was headed toward the audience. As he approached, the boys in the crowd went wild, high-fiving him and calling his name. He didn't leave them hanging, but he didn't stop to talk either. Instead he went straight to the row where his mom, Val, and Stuart were sitting. Of course! He was telling on me. Well, I couldn't exactly blame him.

His mom listened as he said something, nodded, then reached into her purse. A minute later, Bradley marched back toward me.

"Oday," he said with a sigh.

"Oday?" I asked, confused.

"Yeah. I'm oday. My mom had some addergy stuff id her purse. I can addeady feel id working."

"One minute, people," a crew member said.

"Yeah, but—" I wanted to explain to him that I knew how *all the things* I'd done were wrong and mean—sneaky and underhanded, even. And how I never should have doubted his friendship.

"We bodd did stuff we shouldn't hadd," he said,

as if reading my mind. "I should hadd just told you that I wanted to be on the show in the first place, and that I was pladding to go to Shane's party. Anyway, we can talk about that stuff later," he said. "Right now, we've got a show to fiddish."

Then Bradley took one of his palms, rubbed it vigorously in his armpit, and held it out to me.

"Sweat swear," he explained when I looked puzzled. "It's the only thidd more sacred than a spit swear."

"Did you just make that up?" I asked, eyeing his palm suspiciously.

He shrugged.

"Because it's kind of gross."

He shrugged again, this time with an added smile.

"Thirty seconds. Places, please!" one of the *Smarty Pants* crew members called.

Then again, what was a little grossness between best friends? I rubbed my palm in my own armpit and held it out. We shook on it.

"Absolutely and defidditely fair and square from here on out, okay?" Bradley said.

I nodded. Then I breathed a sigh of relief. I had

Bradley back, and with my best friend by my side, I could face anything.

"Welcome back to the final round of *Smarty Pants!*" Mitch shouted. "Are you ready for your last challenge, Clara and Bradley?"

We looked at each other and smiled.

"YEAH!" we both said, raising our fists in the air. Both the girls and the boys went insane cheering.

"Our final category is 'Arts and Culture,'" Mitch said. "And the topic is … " I held my breath and crossed my fingers. "'Super Superheroes.'"

I pumped my fist in the air again. If anyone knew superheroes, it was me.

"Step this way and select your superhero costume from the boxes," Mitch said. "And don't forget your safety goggles. Your final challenge today will be"—he paused as the curtains parted—"to complete this super-hard superhero obstacle course."

A fake cityscape was revealed, complete with crumbling buildings and smoking sewers. "The evil villain, Captain Dumbbell, has unleashed his wrath on the city of Smarty Pants," Mitch said. A cardboard cutout of Captain Dumbbell popped up at the finish line. "It will be up to our two heroes to stop him in time by making their way through the ruined city, scaling ledges, climbing ladders, and swinging between buildings."

While Mitch spoke, Bradley and I were both rifling through the costume boxes, putting together the most awesome superhero costumes possible.

"As you work your way through the course, you'll answer challenging trivia questions. But beware! Get an answer wrong and Captain Dumbbell is sure to seek revenge. Are you prepared, brave heroes?"

Bradley was having a hard time getting his cape tied, so—because my extra-awesome costume was already complete—I went over to help him.

"Ouch!" I said as something hard rubbed between my toes. Of course! Momo's lucky pennies. I sat down on the stage and yanked off my shoe, then pulled one of the coins out. It had some toe jam on it, but I knew Bradley wouldn't mind.

"Momo said to give you this." I pressed it into his palm right before I tied up his cape. "For good luck."

He smiled and tucked it into his own sock.

Before we knew it, the buzzer sounded and we were off. The first challenge was to climb a rope ladder to the top of one of the pretend buildings. There was nothing to it, really.

"Clara, to which superhero league do Batman, Superman, and Wonder Woman belong? Is it: A—the Avengers, B—the Crime Busters, C—the Justice League of America, or D—Aqua Teen Hunger Force?"

Everyone who knows comics knows that Batman, Superman, and Wonder Woman make up the Justice League of America! "C," I said.

DING!

"That's correct!"

Bradley and I both reached the tops of our ladders at the same time and started to run across the roof of the building. From there, red arrows showed us that we were supposed to drop down and scale the window ledge one floor below. With a thousand dollars on the line, neither one of us hesitated.

"Bradley," Mitch said as we lowered ourselves carefully onto the ledge, "Sinestro is the foil, or

archenemy, of which famous superhero? Is it: A—
the Green Lantern, B—Spider-Man, C—Wonder
Woman, or D—She-Ra, Princess of Power?"

I didn't envy Bradley. The answer was A, but the
Green Lantern was an older comic book hero, and
not everyone was familiar with his adventures.
Plus the ledge we were standing on was barely
two inches wide. It took nearly all my focus just
to keep my balance.

"A," Bradley said, probably taking a guess.
"The Green Lantern." Then he took a flying leap
sideways and landed sprawled on the roof of a
pretend building to our left. He raised one hand
in the air to let everyone know he was okay, and
the boys cheered.

DING!

"That is correct!" Mitch said. "Clara, all
superheroes have alter egos. Wonder Woman's real
name is Diana. But what is her surname, or last
name? Is it: A—Prince, B—Princess, C—Amigo,
or D—Flamingo?"

Superman was Clark Kent (everyone knew that)
and Spider-Man was Peter Parker. But Wonder
Woman? Obviously, I knew she had an alter ego,

but what was it? I'd never been the biggest fan. (It always bugged me that you could see the outline of her invisible airplane. I mean, hello! That makes it a clear airplane, not an invisible airplane!) And while all this was going through my mind, I was busy trying to figure out how I was going to make it onto the roof of the pretend building where Bradley had just landed.

I eyed the countdown clock nervously. I only had five seconds to make my choice.

"B—Princess," I said, making a guess. Then before I could lose my nerve, I took a flying leap off the window ledge and landed with a thud on top of the building.

BZZZZZT.

"I'm sorry, Clara, but that is incorrect," Mitch said.

I looked up just in time to see a stream of pudding start shooting out the top of the dunce hat that Captain Dumbbell was wearing.

"Uuuuuuugh," I shouted as green slime hit me square in the safety goggles.

"The correct answer is A—Prince," Mitch said.

Of course! Now that I heard it, I couldn't believe I'd got it wrong.

Still, I didn't have time to let it get me down. I started toward the crisscrossed wires that Bradley was already navigating through. He came out well ahead of me but stopped cold when he saw the next part of the challenge. A crew member was waiting to help him into a safety harness, which was a good thing, because the red arrows painted on the rooftop led to … well, nowhere.

"Bradley," Mitch said, "what power does the superhero called Jean Grey (aka Phoenix) possess? Is it: A—the power of flight, B—the power of telepathy, C—the power of immortality, or D—the power to manipulate energy?"

Phoenix? I could picture her cool white eyes and her red-and-gold suit. I knew the answer, but did Bradley?

As he stood on the ledge considering his options, I navigated through the last of the crisscrossed wires and came to stand beside him. I got into my safety harness, then tiptoed to the edge to look over. It was a loooong way down—and instead of a mat to cushion our fall, there was a giant pool of green slime. Did they seriously expect us to leap from one building to the finish line on the next when they were so far apart?

Bradley must have felt the same, because he wasn't making any move to jump.

"Phoenix," he was muttering to himself. "Phoenix."

I was almost positive he was going to say C, immortality. It would be the logical guess. But instead …

"B," he said. "Telepathy!"

DING!

"That is correct!" Mitch announced.

Bradley was five points ahead—but the game still wasn't over! If he managed to make the leap across the pit of green slime to the finish, he'd score an extra five points, putting him firmly in first place. But if he didn't make it and I did, we'd be tied and would have to battle it out in a lightning round.

I knew I should back up, run, and give it all I had, but the more I looked at the big drop-off, the more I wasn't so sure I could do it.

Bradley peered over the ledge again, shifting his weight back and forth, then he stopped and glanced back at me with a decidedly sick look on his face.

"You've got ten seconds left on the clock, Bradley and Clara," Mitch reminded us oh-so-helpfully. "Can they leap across the pit of slime to defeat Captain Dumbbell?"

"Go for it!" someone in the audience shouted.

"Jump!" someone else hollered.

I took a deep breath and ran forward a few steps, only to stop cold at the edge. It was just too far.

"Hey," Bradley said. He held out his hand. "Do it together?"

"Okay," I said. Honestly, I didn't think I could do it alone.

Hand in hand, we walked back to the far edge of the building so we'd get the longest running start possible.

"Ready?" he asked.

There were five seconds left on the clock. I nodded, and then we ran like we've never run before, leapt into thin air … and …

Fell.

Directly into the pool of slime.

We came up spluttering, still holding hands. I wiped the slime from my goggles with my free hand and looked toward the scoreboard.

I felt my heart sink.
It was official.

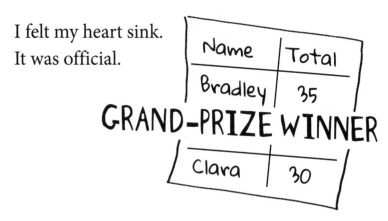

Name	Total
Bradley	35
Clara	30

GRAND-PRIZE WINNER

The biggest dream of my life had *not* come true.
I hadn't won *Smarty Pants*.

I wasn't taking home the one thousand dollars
that would lead me to comic book publishing
fame. Also, I had slime in my mouth—even though
it was really only vanilla pudding dyed green.

The boys in the crowd were going insane,
chanting, "BRADLEY, BRADLEY, BRADLEY!"
But when I looked over at my best friend, he wasn't
looking at them—he was looking at *me*.

I held up my hand for a high-five and he high-
fived me back with a puddingy smack. And that
was when I realized that Momo was right: we
couldn't both win *Smarty Pants*, but that didn't
mean we weren't both lucky.

A Peace Offering

Cats and dogs … in some ways, they're very different animals. For example, one bounds into the room and does a wiggly-waggly dance when its owner comes home, while the other maybe glances up from the couch before going back to sleep. One wags its tail like crazy to show pleasure, while the other wags its tail menacingly when it's about to pounce on its prey and murder it.

But despite those differences, they also share some common ground. They both love food, both hog the best sun spots on the couch, both fear the vacuum cleaner … and the list goes on. In fact, when you really stop to think about it, cats and dogs are alike in more ways than they're different, and there's no reason they can't get along—at least, most of the time.

In the weeks after the *Smarty Pants* crew packed up and left town, most things went back to normal.

Bradley and I stopped studying at every possible second and returned to digging holes and drawing comics. I finished @*Cat: Doggy Decimator*, and Bradley said it was his number-one favorite @Cat adventure so far.

Bradley liked it so much, in fact, that he kept trying to convince me to let him use his prize money to publish it. But there was no way I was agreeing to that. After all, he'd won the thousand dollars fair and square.

"Not exactly," he said. "I didn't know the last answer for sure. I just took a guess!"

But taking guesses was part of the game. And as it happened, "Never be afraid to take chances" was the last of Stuart's Six Secrets to Success—which, in the end, had served Bradley pretty well.

In fact, ever since he'd won *Smarty Pants*, my best friend was like a different person. For one thing, he'd become a bit of a celebrity. Sarah Barrasson interviewed him on the six o'clock news. She asked him all about the experience and called him a role model for the kids of Gleason. And for once, he didn't seem to mind the spotlight so much. In fact, once he got a taste of it, he kind of enjoyed it.

We still watched *Smarty Pants* every day after school too, but we didn't laugh quite so loudly at Mitch O'Toole's puns, since we knew they were all scripted. Plus something about knowing how mean he was in real life made everything he did less funny.

After the final filming finished, Bradley and I started a letter-writing campaign, trying to tell the show's executives how unfair Mitch was to his assistant, Mario. We were hoping we could get Mario his job back, but all our letters went unanswered. In the end, though, things worked out for the best.

Bradley—with his amazing attention to detail—was the one who spotted Mario outside the mushroom house. It happened when Bradley's little sister, Val, was watching a baby show called *Fantasy Fables* while we were doing our homework on the rug.

"Is that—?" Bradley put his math book down. "It is! Look, Clara! Mario's on TV!"

It was true. There he was, stomping his feet and skipping in circles to a song about friendship, dressed like an elf!

Instead of his usual stooped shoulders and sad eyes, Mario was standing tall and looking … well, there was no other word for it: spritely. He grinned as the tip of his pointy hat flopped from side to side in time with his merry steps.

"I guess he already found a new job," I said.

"And he looks pretty happy about it," Bradley observed.

We both watched in wonder as Mario twirled under a magical rainbow that sprayed sparkles in all directions. "Happy" was putting it mildly.

But even though Mario was thriving and Bradley and I were friends again, there was one thing that didn't end well: the boys and girls at Gledhill Elementary were still fighting like cats and dogs.

One day, the boys stole some of the girls' skipping ropes and tied them in knots, so the girls retaliated by letting all the air out of the boys' volleyballs. To get back at them, the boys butted in line and took all the freezies at the school BBQ. So the girls retaliated by hiding every last pair of scissors so they couldn't cut them open.

And even though the yard monitors and teachers kept trying to get the kids to talk it out and be nice to each other, no amount of detentions or calls to parents seemed to be doing the trick.

"This sucks," Bradley said one day at recess, about two weeks after the show had finished. We were sitting at a picnic table, trying to steer clear of some name-calling going on between

Bossy Becky and the girls and Shane Biggs and the boys. The girls still had total control over the monkey bars, while the boys wouldn't let a single girl on the climber, and if someone approached the wrong area, he or she was sure to get chased away. Besides the picnic tables, there really was no neutral territory anymore.

"Yeah," I said, "it totally sucks." I scratched my head and went back to the list we were making. It was a bunch of ideas for how Bradley could spend his prize money, which was still just sitting in his bank account.

Things to buy with $1,000!
- HUGE candy shopping spree
- Go-kart
- Electric skateboard
- Rare fossil
- Deluxe tree house

"I mean, don't get me wrong—the monkey bars are rusty, and the climber is so babyish. But I kind of miss being able to use them. The picnic table's getting boring," I said.

"Totally boring," Bradley agreed, taking the list

from me and reading it over.

"I wish there was something we could do to make them stop fighting," I added miserably.

"Wait a second!" Bradley grabbed my pen and, in his neat, careful handwriting, added an idea to the bottom of the list.

Funds for this playground were generously donated by Bradley D. and the Gledhill Elementary School Council.

"What do you think?" he asked.

"I don't know. That would be *really* expensive. There'd be no money left over."

He shrugged. "So?"

I grinned at him. Not only was my best friend smart, thoughtful, brave, and noble, but he was always looking out for the common good … which was about all a cool cat like me could ask for in a sidekick—no, wait, I mean *co-hero and best friend*.

And just like that, the age-old battle between the boys and the girls ended peacefully.

@Cat and Poodle Noodle exchange peace offerings
… or do they?

Well, okay … not really. But Bradley and I never broke our sweat swear to stay best friends, and at least we had a super-deluxe jungle gym with a twirly slide. So that was definitely something.

THE END